WHATEVER HAPPENED TO WHITNEY LAKE?

Copyright © 2022 by Angie Koenig Olson

All rights reserved. The reproduction or utilization of this work in whole or in part in any form by any electronic or mechanical or other means is forbidden without the express permission of the author.

olsonangie8@gmail.com

ISBN: 9798752031762

Whitney's mind was never settled, but filled with images of remote and exotic destinations. She'd often close her eyes and feel a warm soft breeze brushing across her face, while palm trees swayed gently above her on some distant Caribbean-Island. Other times, she would be swishing down a steep mountain slope high up in the Alps of Austria or Switzerland.

It was all there in her head — this imaginary life. Someday, this would be her life, she just knew it to be true.

Suddenly, all her dreams and visions miraculously become true when a chance stranger appears and turns her life into one that so far she had only imagined.

Whitney finds herself in a whirlwind of alien adventure, a cautious romance, and unforeseen deception.

A Novel

Part I

BE CAREFUL WHAT YOU WISH FOR

Chapter 1

There was a light knock on her apartment door. She knew it was him, Aidan somebody. Up until now, she had called him Mr. Portillo. She hesitated, took a deep breath, while nervously brushing a strand of hair behind her left ear; then she opened the door.

"Hello," said Whitney.

"Hello to you, Stewardess Girl."

"You never asked my name, although my last name was on my uniform when you were on my flight today.

"My name is Whitney, Whitney Lake."

"And I am Aidan, Mr. Portillo to you."

He quickly stepped inside with a broad smile on his tanned face, and asked if she was ready to go? He looked so handsome with his crisp white shirt and navy jacket. Whitney felt a little uneasy and not as confident as she usually was. She felt herself fidgeting around as she grabbed a sweater that she had placed on the chair next to her apartment door, knowing that restaurants are usually chilly in the evening.

They left her apartment and walked past some residents who were still lollygagging around the pool. It was mostly singles who lived in the complex, at least that is what she had been told when she rented her one bedroom about a year prior. That really didn't matter much to her. Whitney liked to keep to herself. She was hoping to slip by the pool and not see the date that she had cancelled, just a couple of hours ago. But there he was, still sitting by the pool, reclining in a lounge chair. When the lounger saw them, strolling side-by-side, his eyes were spewing sparks as he called Whitney a bunch of names.

"Let's go," said Whitney, as she tugged on Aidan's arm to move him along at a faster-pace. She felt she had to tell Mr. Portillo that this fellow was one of the reasons that she had to decide about dinner with him. He shrugged his shoulders as if to say, who cares—I am the one she chose tonight. She suddenly felt she was giving up some of herself; some of her forever guarded life. Whitney had spent all of her teen and young adult years avoiding serious relationships. Her stomach was uneasy, thinking and wondering if this guy would be the one to spin her into a new life. *No, no, no, I must remain in control.*

~

He was the perfect gentleman, making sure she stepped before him, opening his Lincoln's car door, and asking at the same time, if she liked Charlie's Exceptional Restaurant. She said he had asked her that before, and again said she did, and that would be great, although she had never had dinner there.

The drive was without hurry, through the outskirts of the city and past the lakes that she had walked around so many times. The sun was still shining, but hidden by the taller apartment buildings that skirted the avenue. Whitney nervously chatted about why she liked this part of the city, while Mr. Portillo politely nodded at most every comment she made.

Whitney asked if he had ever had a date with a stewardess before?

Aidan answered with a brief hesitation, "No, not that I know of."

Whitney wondered what exactly that meant, "not that I know of," but didn't pursue it. *Am I just another number to him?* she wondered.

When they arrived at the restaurant, the hostess summoned Charlie, and Charlie graciously led them to one of the finest tables, and brought the chair out for Whitney to sit, placing the linen napkin across her lap, just as she had been taught at Patricia Stevens Finishing School. Charlie chatted with them and asked what they would like to drink? Whitney leaned forward, she hadn't noticed Aidan's piercing blue eyes before, as he asked her if she liked martinis? Gin or vodka? She was so mesmerized by his eyes, that when he asked her a second time, she jumped a little from her chair, and came out of her trance and finally blurted out, "Gin, sure, that would be wonderful," as she sat back and took a deep breath.

Whitney slowly sipped the harsh clear liquid for about an hour or so, leaving the olive resting in the bottom of the stemmed glass. Mr. Portillo hadn't eaten his olive, and she wasn't sure if she should eat it or not. She thought maybe it was just for flavor. She was finally feeling more relaxed and at ease. Maybe it was the effects of the martini, or just maybe it was the relaxed nature of Mr. Portillo that calmed her spirit; more than she had felt with anyone else.

The hours seem to slip by, first savoring a shrimp cocktail, and then a well-done end-cut of prime rib. This was one of the first dates she had had on which she found herself not fidgeting and wanting the evening to be over as soon as possible. They talked about travel and many of the destinations that he had bobbed in and out of, and would enjoy returning to again: Europe, South America, the Caribbean Islands, just to name a few. Whitney's head was swimming, thinking this was his everyday lifestyle. In the back of her mind, she was thinking, *seeing the world.* Those were the words that kept spinning in her mind. *He has been seeing the world.* At the same time, she didn't want him to think that she hadn't been anywhere, so she had to mention some of the cities that she had been to with NWA such as New York, Miami, Chicago and Seattle. Her travels seem so trivial compared to where he had been. He had traveled all over the world. Whitney couldn't stop thinking: *The Universe must have brought him to me.*

By the time they returned to her apartment, it was close to midnight. He walked her to the door and stepped inside as Whitney said good night and thanked him for the lovely dinner and interesting conversation. She told him that she had to fly the next afternoon, and that she needed to get her rest. His eyes scanned around her modest apartment and then he said, "You don't have a television."

Whitney said, "I don't watch TV, so I don't have one." She didn't want him to think that she couldn't afford a TV if she really wanted one.

With that, he said good night, and said he would call her soon.

Chapter 2

Whitney's weekly schedule was mostly three days flying and three days home. A week went by, then two, then three, and no word from Mr. Portillo. So, she put him out of her mind and really sort of forgot about him. Then one night, shortly after she returned home from a trip, the phone rang, and it was him. He said he had been out of the country on business, and had just returned the day before. He asked, "Would you like to go flying tomorrow?"

"Flying," she said, "I fly for my work."

Aidan said, "This is different. Not like flying in a commercial jet for work."

In Aidan's somewhat arrogant fashion, he continued instructing Whitney.

"This is *real* flying," he said, "I'll show you what it is *really* like to fly. Tomorrow is going to be such a beautiful day, and I thought we would fly around the lakes and rivers in the area. I'll pick you up at 8am. Flying is best in the early part of the day. The winds are usually calm before the sun warms the air. And, the air is also the clearest just after dawn. We should be able to almost see forever."

Whitney knew about the calm and clear air, after all she had been flying with NWA for almost three years. But she let him be the teacher, rather than saying, 'I know that'. She really wanted him to know that she knew about the morning air being calm and clearest. Somehow, she felt a bit like a child with him.

And so that is what they did. Whitney hadn't been in a small airplane before, but it really wasn't that small. When she had first met Mr. Portillo on the flight coming back from Miami, he told her he flew his own plane, so Whitney went to the library and researched the Cessna so as not to appear too naïve.

His plane was a twin-engine Cessna with six passengers' seats. He picked her up at her St. Louis Park apartment and they drove to a terminal on the north side of the main airport that was for private aircraft only. Everyone seemed to know him, and the Cessna was out of the hanger, fueled, and ready for them to board as soon as they arrived.

He handed her a headset and motioned her to sit in the co-pilot's seat. She buckled her seatbelt as Aidan revved the engines at the end of the runway. They were cleared for takeoff, and up and away they went, just as smooth as silk. They flew over the tallest buildings in downtown St. Paul, up and down the lazy Mississippi, and over the rocky banks of the shimmering St. Croix River. The Cessna glided effortlessly, across the downtown Minneapolis skyline, and over Lake Minnetonka, with its endless bays, and over a hundred miles of shoreline. It was a crystal-clear day, and the land and lakes all appeared to be so quiet and peaceful. Every now and then, Mr. Portillo would glance over to her. Whitney thought he was looking to see if she was enjoying the sights and the ride. He was pleased to see the smile on her face—that said it all.

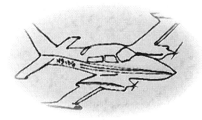

They landed smoothly back at the Minneapolis airport in early afternoon. He drove her back to her apartment and said, "I will call you."

Whitney thought, *I've heard that before*. As far as she was concerned, maybe it was best that this relationship remained at arms' length.

Chapter 3

Whitney was off to work the next day for one of her usual three-day-sprints. While driving home from the airport, she was feeling a little peopled-out. She often felt like she needed some quiet-time by herself after three days inside a tube with hundreds of strangers.

When she opened her apartment door, her jaw dropped with surprise. There sitting in the middle of her living room was the biggest console TV that she had ever seen. *There is only one person who could have sent this to my apartment, she thought*. Needless to say, she was surprised and annoyed as she marched down to the apartment house manager and asked who delivered this monster to her apartment.

The manager said, "Sorry, it was a delivery service and I don't know any more than that. The delivery guy was told to just leave it."

It could only be one person; the guy with the Cessna. How dare he do that, when I told him that I didn't watch TV, or I would have one.

~

It was a week or so later, when Aidan telephoned Whitney. She immediately questioned him about the TV. His answer was that maybe he would want to watch TV when he was at her apartment. He didn't seem to be bothered that she firmly questioned him. In fact, she sensed pleasure in his voice. She wasn't planning for him to stay at her apartment for any length of time!

She didn't thank him. She felt his so-called generosity was an imposition on her.

What Ever Happened to Whitney Lake?

Whitney didn't hear from Aidan again for a couple of weeks, so she assumed he had gone off somewhere on business, or maybe with someone else. By now, she had moved a few things around in her apartment and had someone help her move the monster TV to a wall where it wouldn't be so conspicuous. It was so far from her taste in furniture, and the size—that awful size—it was like a giant white elephant.

Chapter 4

When Whitney's phone rang several days later, it was Aidan, and he explained that he had once again been out of the country for about two weeks. He then asked if she would like to fly to New Orleans and stay in the French Quarter and eat raw oysters at his favorite oyster bar. He said that he had business in New Orleans and they could leave the next day after she returned from her working flight. How could she refuse? This sounded so enticing! And so, she said, "Sure I would love to go to New Orleans." NWA did not fly there currently, so it was somewhere that Whitney had not yet discovered.

~

They flew the Cessna to Louis Armstrong Airport in New Orleans, with one fuel stop in Saint Louis, Missouri. Aidan had made a reservation at the classic Bourbon Orleans Hotel that was walking distance from the French Quarter.

When they walked up to the check-in desk, the lady behind the desk, looked at Aidan and then at Whitney, and looked down at the desk with a smile. Whitney knew what she was thinking—isn't she a little young to be with this man? But the clerk didn't say a word and allowed Aidan to sign in. The clerk summoned a boy to take their bags to the room. Whitney was a little nervous about being with Aidan in a strange hotel and an unfamiliar city.

However, Aidan was the perfect gentleman. As soon as their luggage was brought to their room, he suggested they find an outdoor café on Bourbon Street for a late lunch.

The tables were all small at the cafés, and hardly room for a leisure time as the avenue was filling with tourists and jazz music was drifting into the street from every direction. The sun was just sneaking behind the quaint French buildings as they strolled along, having to watch each step in Whitney's high-heels on the uneven cobblestones. Whitney realized that she was experiencing Aidan's lifestyle as he told her that the next stop would be Felix's; his favorite oyster bar.

Whitney said, "Sure, I'll try oysters, seems like the thing to do in New Orleans."

White ceramic tile covered the floors, walls and ceiling of the oyster bar. Whitney was thinking that they must hose-down the entire place every night to keep it smelling as fresh as the sea as it did. With no more than a dozen tables, the bar was almost filled with oyster-loving-men.

What Ever Happened to Whitney Lake?

Whitney looked around and noticed that she was the only female in the place. *Interesting, she thought.*

They found an empty high-topped table to lean against, ordered a tall beer, and watched the big hands of the oysterman behind the counter as he slid a sharp steel-point into an oyster and cracked open the chilled shells, then dropped them on a plate, as it skated across the counter. Whitney watched Aidan as he spooned some horseradish and catsup onto the oyster, opened his mouth wide, and let it slide down his throat, grabbed a couple of crackers, and finished with a big gulp of beer. Whitney wasn't sure if she could swallow that large of a slimy thing all at once. She politely asked the oyster man if he could pick out the smallest ones for her, she was told that you don't chew the oyster but swallow it whole. He frowned a little and mumbled under his breath as he sorted through the pile of craggy looking shells that were piled in front of him.

She ate her first half-dozen raw oysters with horseradish and catsup, many crackers, and a mug of local tap-beer.

She had no idea how slithery and slimy they would be. But, she did it, and could check it off her list of must-do. The no chewing, she was told, is because the oyster is still alive as it slithers down your throat.

It sounded just awful to her, when she thought about it, and was not sure if she wanted to do the oyster bar again.

~

The next day, Whitney lazily strolled through the narrow streets of the French Quarter alone, stopping here and there, listening to the jazz music floating out into the streets, from the many open doors of bars. Aidan had disappeared right after breakfast and said that he would be back later in the afternoon.

That evening, they ate sumptuous creole crab and shrimp at the Orleans Hotel, and slowly danced to the smooth New Orleans Jazz. Whitney realized how good Aidan's arms felt around her waist and torso. He had a soft pleasing smile that stayed as they strolled down to the marketplace for French Beignets at the Café Beignet on Royal Street. The sweet aroma of the delicate French pastry seemed to penetrate the air for blocks around. The basket of hot Beignets were fresh out of the fryer, then dusted with powdered sugar and served with a strong cup of New Orleans famous chicory coffee.

~

They left New Orleans after three days of roaming around the French Quarters. Whitney needed to get back to Minneapolis, she was scheduled to fly the next day. She liked the independence of having her own job, and felt when she left on a trip with NWA, she was flying off to her own personal freedom.

It was a lovely time in New Orleans. There was definitely something very interesting about this man. It seemed as if he floated in and out of her life, with the last words always being, "I'll call you." He never called to just say hello, or to just chat on the phone. He only called if he wanted to go to dinner, or to fly off somewhere. He was definitely intriguing. But she knew very little about him. He kept his personal life to himself, and she was careful not to ask him questions, that way she didn't have to talk about her personal life either. This was the perfect arrangement for her.

~

One winter evening, they were standing in line inside the entry of a local restaurant in the western Twin Cities. Aidan turned to Whitney and said, "Let's go," as he nudged her towards the restaurant's door. He couldn't get out the door fast enough. Whitney had known Aidan for a few months now, and this was the first time he didn't want to be seen with Whitney.

They drove back to the city and found a restaurant for dinner. Aidan was quiet, until they sat down at a corner-table away from the other diners. It was time for an owning up of his situation. With his sandy-haired head lowered, and not looking at Whitney, he confessed that he was legally married, but his wife lived in Arizona most of the year, and they were separated. It was obvious to Whitney that he saw someone that he didn't want to see, *with her.* Whitney told him that she wasn't surprised, it was unlikely that someone like him would be unattached. It was also very unusual for anyone to be traveling around the world, it seemed like weekly, and to have a family of any kind. He didn't mention any children or anything else about his private life. Although Whitney didn't like the fact that a stray wife was somewhere in the picture, it seemed of little concern to him.

Aidan said, "She is well taken care of."

In some ways Whitney thought that his marital situation left her off the hook. With this news, he wouldn't be pressuring Whitney to settle down, like so many of her friends and also family members.

Chapter 5

But Whitney was wrong. Even if Aidan was legally attached, he was still becoming more insistent that she give up her airline job, making comments like, "You are better than that job, and besides you don't need it, I will take care of you." She wasn't sure what that exactly meant to him, but she knew what it meant to her. It meant, to give up all that she had worked for and hung onto up until now. Would she ever be able to convince him how far she had come and that she just couldn't turn back?

Maybe he would understand if she told him about her childhood, and maybe about her mother. All she had ever talked about with Aidan, was her job at NWA and traveling.

~

The day finally came for Whitney to move into her new home in St. Louis Park. Two strong friends backed a trailer up to her apartment and loaded what furniture she had in her one-bedroom flat. And then, there was the giant TV. "Where did that monster come from?" asked a friend. She just said, "Never mind, it is a long story, and

I don't want to get into that tale at the moment." Her friends just shook their heads and smiled. "It certainly must be a good story," said one of the boys.

She was excited about the move, and couldn't wait to decorate and make it her home. With the frequent traveling with Aidan, she had so little time to just be by herself. Before she met Aidan, Whitney relished her alone time, especially after a working flight. Somehow, he didn't really fit into her current picture. Now here she was, settling into her cozy house, with little thought of Aidan fitting into her life right then.

Whitney started turning Aidan down when he wanted to fly out of town as soon as she returned from her working-trips. "I need a day to be by myself," she would say. He didn't really like the fact that she was pushing him away, but he didn't have a choice, if he wanted her to be in his life. From their first date, Whitney had sensed that he was accustomed to getting his own way and was not used to resistance.

Aidan also expressed his thoughts about her buying a one-bedroom house, saying that he thought it was a poor investment. Whitney didn't' think he thought she should buy a house at all, for that matter. They were apparently on completely different life-paths. The age difference was beginning to be more obvious to Whitney. No one Whitney's age could financially support Mr. Portillo's life-style. She was busy enjoying her single life, and he felt just the opposite, wanting her to settle down and be satisfied with just him. On occasion, he would also bring up having a child together, saying that they would have a lifetime bond from then on.

Some words rang sharp to her mind—*be satisfied with him*. Aidan would often say matter-of-factly, "I am all you will ever need. Leave the airline and your flying friends behind."

It brought to mind the words of a sunbathing boy at the pool saying, "You are getting old, and no boys are going to want a girl as old as you."

Was that really true? Was twenty-five over the hill?

Or, Whitney's sibling saying; "When are you going to settle down, get married and raise a family, and stop running around the world?"

Never, Whitney said to herself. *I will never be complacent and satisfied.* Somehow, Mr. Portillo brought back images that she had long ago forgotten, or maybe had just shoved way back in her memories. All she really wanted more than anything was to remain self-reliant and not have to depend financially on anyone.

Whitney tried her best to keep to herself in her one-bedroom hide-a-way, but Mr. Portillo wouldn't let her alone, and started sending workmen over to remodel her house while she was away on trips. Slowly, without her realizing what was happening, he was taking control of her life, even wanting to take her to the airport for her scheduled trips, and pick her up when she returned a few days later. That seemed like such a nice jester on Aidan's part, thinking that she had door to door service, and didn't have concerns about the cold weather or rain or even the wind. He started making more comments about her not needing any of the people that she worked with, or for that matter any friends, only him. The ladies sure had an eye for him. As a matter of fact, some of the girls that Whitney worked with would ooooh, and ahhhh, when they saw Mr. Portillo, and say to let them know if she was ever finished with him.

Whitney had to admit, he was very attractive with his custom fitting slacks and sport coat. And, always a crisp white tailored shirt that contrasted with his forever tan face. His tall, thin and in-shape body boasted of confidence that seemed to disarm whomever came in contact with him. It was quite obvious to Whitney that Aidan was a magnet to the ladies. He had a style and look about him that was exactly what attracted Whitney that day when they met on her flight from Miami.

~

What Ever Happened to Whitney Lake?

If their relationship was going to blossom into more than being traveling companions, Whitney wanted to know more about Aidan, and she thought if she talked about her past, that he would have a better understanding of who she really was, and maybe he would talk about himself as well. It was a long-shot to Whitney because Aidan had little or no concern about anything in the past.

Whitney said she had made a pact with herself not to have the same life as her mother, and so far she had been successful. Her mother had been held captive in a life dependent on someone else for her survival and the welfare of her eight children. Whitney had no intention of repeating her mother's entrapment.

Aiden seemed to fidget around as she was talking, as if he didn't want to hear any of this. It seemed he just wanted her to be a robot and not be personal about who she was. He wanted her to be the way *he* wanted her to be. So, they continued traveling together, most times Whitney thought that this was the best of both worlds

~

Aidan never mentioned the conversation again, but seemed to look at Whitney differently after that time.

Whitney didn't think that he was interested in any of her life before him. He lived in the moment, and many times she felt as if she was traveling with a stranger. Other times, Whitney realized that she seemed to be losing a little more of herself and becoming more of just *Aidan's girl*.

Chapter 6

They traveled to Miami, mostly just for the day, for those shopping trips where he watched her try on clothes that he liked and gave his nod of approval. Most of the clothes at this store were for older women, and Whitney knew that she would not be wearing any of the clothes. She'd graciously thank him for all the purchases, and when she'd arrive back home, stuff the packages in the back of the closet for a while; little by little, they would make their way to a thrift store. Whitney often wondered what he was thinking—he knew that she was twenty-some-years younger than him, and she didn't at all care for that Jewish clothing store that he frequented.

As it was, Whitney still found herself saying yes, to a trip to New York for a Broadway show, or for a quick overnight to the Florida beaches for a day in the sun, or wherever the wind would take them.

~

They traveled to Mexico in search of the Teotihuacan Aztec ruins near Mexico City, and ventured on to Acapulco where they stayed at the posh Las Brisas Resort, known for the celebrities who frequented it. Whitney and Aidan relaxed by their private pool that overlooked the quiet waters of Acapulco Bay. Each morning, fresh fruit and hot rolls were delivered to their suite. When they checked in, Aidan was handed the keys to a pink striped golf cart. It was supposed to be used on the resort's property only, but Aiden took liberties and drove it down the hillside and into the main part of town.

~

While having lunch at the pool restaurant, a film crew arrived with Dean Martin to film one of his Matt Helm movies. They didn't ask Aidan and Whitney to leave the area, but instead they were encouraged to stay and watch the filming—maybe they would be off in a distance in the film. As it was, it was more time than they cared to spend, after watching many film retakes. The female star was positioned close to the sea wall and with the cameras rolling she was supposed to playfully interact with Mr. Martin. After the first three camera-rolls she was soaked by the waves smashing against the rock wall, and the makeup crew would take half an hour redoing the star for another take.

They found filming to be quite boring, so they drove the pink-jeep down to the other end of town where the cliff divers were performing most of the afternoon. Some of the divers seemed to be professional, and others would dive for a few pesos from any-one of the tourists. Aidan gave several pesos to a young boy who looked to be no more than twelve. He scampered up the rock wall barefoot, and jumped from the high cliff without hesitation, then was quickly back asking for more pesos.

"Once was enough," said Aidan, as he held onto Whitney's arm and led her back out into the street. "These kids will jump off that cliff many times for a few pesos." It was like Aidan had had enough of that, and wanted to move on. He never seemed to ask Whitney what she thought. He always knew best.

~

That evening, they dined at the mountain-top restaurant of the Las Brisas while Mexican guitars softly serenaded them under the star-studded sky. They swayed on the dance floor to the intoxicating music with

a gentle breeze brushing across Whitney's face. She remembered imagining this moment, long before she had met Aidan. Whitney looked up at Aidan as he smiled down at her and said, "I need you to be with me always."

Whitney wondered what Aidan meant by what he said, but she decided to brush it off as the atmosphere of the night, and thought he would have forgotten what he said by morning.

What Ever Happened to Whitney Lake?

~

The next day, Aidan asked Whitney if she would like to go scuba diving with him. She said she had not ventured into diving before, and was not a particularly good swimmer, and she wasn't really interested in going into the ocean without any training. "No problem," said Aidan. "I will arrange for a diver/instructor to take us out in a boat."

They strolled down the beach to a dive hut and Aidan went inside to make the arrangements. Whitney doubted if he told the instructor that she wasn't a good swimmer.

In no-time, the equipment was loaded into a rustic old dive boat that they had noticed bobbing along in the bay. The boatman swam out to the boat, jumped in, and brought the boat to shore. Aidan and Whitney climbed in at a small dock, and the boat quickly headed out into the water's gentle roll. Aidan apparently had been told about the reef with colorful fish that was located farther out into the big Bay of Acapulco. When the boat finally stopped, the instructor started loading scuba gear onto Whitney without saying a word. As the boatman was pulling straps tight across Whitney, she was becoming more uneasy about this whole adventure.

Aidan seemed quite at ease, or maybe he was just fearless. At that point, Aidan was already in the water. Within a few minutes, the instructor told or pointed for Whitney to sit on the side of the boat, and when he signaled her, to fall over backwards into the water. Being in Mexico, the instructor spoke little English and the little he spoke, was hard to understand.

Whitney said, "But I don't know what to do when I get into the water?"

The instructor said, "No worry, I will tell you what to do once you are in the water."

She followed his instructions, fell backwards into the water. When the water cleared from her mask, she looked around for the trainer and for Aidan. No one was in her sight.

At that point, she was shaking so badly that all she could say to herself was, *I want back in the boat.* Was Aidan testing her, or was he just unconcerned? After all, she was an independent girl who could take care of herself. She slowly swam with the mountain of equipment on her back, and made it to the small ladder that hung on the side of the boat. Whitney edged her way up the boat's side and fell inside. Finally, she calmed herself enough to remove all the heavy gear while the small boat rocked in the ocean swells.

What Ever Happened to Whitney Lake?

The next few hours were spent watching Aidan swim around in utter contentment. Neither Aidan or the so-called-instructor came to see if Whitney needed help, or if they were wondering why she climbed back into the boat. Aidan later said that she missed all the beautiful and very colorful fish that were swimming in and around the reef. Whitney said she needed some training, maybe in a pool before she would tackle a dive again. He had no idea the level of fear that had taken place in Whitney, and it also didn't seem to matter to him. She did willfully go along. She did have a choice, And she could have said no.

Was this a test of some sort? Or, was he just doing what he wanted to do and expected Whitney to not question him about whatever it was that Aidan had on his mind.

It didn't stop there, because the next day, Aidan rented a small sail boat at the shore near town, and they headed out into the bay in mid-morning. The boat was more like a large surf-board that they sat on top of, and had to lay flat as they dodged the sail boom to change direction. At first it seemed delightful, with a soft breeze filling the single sail. They tacked back and forth across the bay for a couple of hours, and then as quickly as the breeze came, it died. The ocean was instantly still, as the tide began pulling the skiff back out to sea. By now, the sun was hot and harsh, and they hadn't brought any cover or lotion to block any of the rays. There they were, bobbing on this skiff, trying to tack to get back to shore, to no avail. They continued to drift farther and farther from shore, and by now, it was late afternoon and the sun was disappearing behind the protruding rocks of the bay. Boats would motor by and not pay much attention to them, and Whitney didn't think Aidan wanted her or anyone else to think that they were in trouble.

Finally, when a fishing boat came by and asked if they needed help getting back to shore, Whitney blurted out, "Yes please, yes we do," not waiting for Aidan to respond. The fisherman threw a rope to them and Aidan tied it to their mast. Whitney was desperate for shade; her skin was now starting to turn bright red from the relentless sun.

That evening, Whitney tried to cool her skin down with towels soaked in ice water. Sleep escaped her as she felt feverish from the deep burns.

Within a few days, Whitney's skin began peeling in sheets. Her raw skin was even unable to permit a touch or a fabric. It was still about a week before she was scheduled to fly for work, so she was hoping she would be healed enough to tolerate her uniform. Aidan did apply some cooling and healing lotion to her back and Whitney did the same for him. Aidan was as fair-skinned as Whitney, but the excess sun did not seem to affect him as much as it did her.

All Aidan said was, "If you didn't still have that job you wouldn't have to worry about the sunburn and about leaving in time to fly." Whitney was getting used to a comment such as this, and chose to ignore it once again.

~

Aidan and Whitney occasionally traveled to Winnipeg Canada for Aidan's business. At first, she was not introduced to anyone who he associated with in Winnipeg, or for that matter, any of his business destinations. Most times Whitney felt like she was the secret girlfriend, and she guessed she really was. Aidan would drop her off at a mall for shopping and stuff some bills in her hand and say, "Go have lunch and I will pick you up in a few hours." Although she enjoyed seeing new cities, she was not much of a shopper, and was more often turning Aidan down when he was only traveling on business.

~

Whitney chose to ignore the closing in by Aidan, and the relinquishing of her freedom for this lifestyle. It was not only becoming very much a part of her life, but in many ways, was *becoming* her life. She was caught in his web, as it became harder and harder to say no, with constant surprises of another exotic place to explore.

Chapter 7

Aidan preferred to pilot his Cessna whenever possible, and their flights were sometimes nerve-wracking to Whitney. On one occasion, they were returning from Puerto Rico, and they had to land for fuel on what appeared to be an almost deserted island somewhere in the archipelago of the Bahamas. The island was flat and almost treeless. except for a few low-growing scrubby shrubs that were leaning away from the prevailing winds. The day was hot and without a whimper of a breeze. They landed on a short coral-packed runway and began to taxi towards a small building when a man sauntered out and motioned the Cessna to stop. Aidan opened his cockpit window and said that he had landed for fuel. The conversation continued for a few minutes, with back-and-forth jabbering. Apparently, there was a landing fee for using the coral strip on this sleepy island. Aidan lowered the steps and hopped down out of the Cessna and got into the suntanned man's sandy car and drove away, leaving Whitney behind with little to no explanation as to when he would return. She waited in the sweltering plane, trying to sit next to the open door but still out of the tropical sun. It was more than an hour later, when Aidan returned and finally a man was told to start fueling. Aidan said that this landing-strip had a surprise landing fee, and that he was escorted into town to pay it to the mayor, with a few hundred extra in the con's pocket to let his plane leave. Aidan knew he was taken advantage of, but brushed it off as nothing unusual. That is when Whitney came to realize that Aidan really liked living on the edge. He was indeed fearless, but also so matter-of-fact about danger of any kind.

~

Another time, when they were returning from the islands, the Cessna was short of fuel, and Aidan had previously filed a flight-plan for a fuel stop in Montgomery, Alabama.

It was just before sunset, and the tumultuous clouds were greenish-black, as they rolled at the edge of the horizon. The lightning pierced down to earth while the sky constantly lit up from the southern heat. There were storms in all directions. Aidan said that he didn't have a choice, the Cessna couldn't make it to an alternate airport; they had to land for fuel.

The Cessna toppled from one side to the other while it dropped a couple hundred feet in down-drafts.

What Ever Happened to Whitney Lake?

Whitney was told to watch-out for the downtown buildings that were somewhere close below. Aidan also told her to look-out for the runway, which was near impossible through the wind and the pounding rain. The visibility was down to nothing.

Finally, the city lights broke through the sheets of rain, and they could see the buildings peeking through the storm. The muted runway lights came into view as Aidan hung on to the wheel of the Cessna for a final approach. He lowered the landing gear just before touching down, as sheets of standing water yanked the plane sideways across the concrete like a cowboy riding a bronco. Whitney was watching Aidan as he stood up to hold on to the steering-wheel. When they finally came to a stop, they could barely see the terminal to taxi in. Somehow, they made it there, and an attendant came out and tied-down the plane. Aidan opened the cabin door and they jumped down the plane's steps and ran to the terminal, with lightning so constant, the night had disappeared.

They were the last plane in because of the weather, with tornados spotted all around Montgomery. The only reason Montgomery allowed the Cessna to land was because the aircraft was short of fuel, and this was the scheduled flight plan that Aidan had filed.

Within a couple of hours, the weather quieted down, the greenish-black clouds rolled on out of the area, and the sky was showing signs of the sun peeking out on the horizon. It took another hour before the water drained off the concrete and the airport runways were back open for takeoffs and landing.

Aidan looked at Whitney and said, "I'll get fueled-up and we'll be ready to go."

Whitney looked back at Aidan and said, "You *are* kidding, right? You can go if you want to. I'm going to a hotel, and I'll take a commercial airline home in the morning. My heart hasn't stopped racing from the storm."

He scoffed a little—he wasn't used to not getting his own way. In the end, he went to the hotel with Whitney and they flew the Cessna back to Minneapolis in the morning.

~

To Aidan, having the Cessna was like owning an auto. It seemed to be quite adequate when flying at lower altitudes, but he became obsessed with more powerful engines. So, he had the engines super-charged so that they could maintain a higher altitude over the mountains. As it was, the super-charged engines would overheat at just about any altitude.

What Ever Happened to Whitney Lake?

On one occasion, they were flying back from Winnipeg and one engine was over-heating when they were over the St. Cloud area. Aidan shut down the hot engine and said that he could make it to the Twin Cities airport on one engine. The temperature of the Cessna's last engine was rising little by little, but Aidan kept insisting that they could make it to the Twin Cities. Aidan never said a word to the tower that they couldn't maintain an altitude. As it was, the Cessna was slowly and involuntarily descending over the downtown St. Paul skyline. The tower had said to maintain a certain altitude on their final approach, and the aircraft just couldn't—and didn't. Again, Aidan never mentioned to the tower that they were in trouble. Whitney never did understand why. Miraculously, they were cleared to land and Aidan landed the Cessna with one dead engine like it was just another day flying, and not anything unusual.

~

The last time Whitney was in that Cessna, they had to land in Grand Forks, North Dakota, because of the overheating engines, again. They had landed there with only one working engine, so he would have to leave the plane there to be repaired or maybe decide what to do. It had become too unreliable. Aidan had a business friend there who also owned a plane and he said he would give them a ride back to the city. When Whitney saw the plane, she said, "You have got to be joking. We can't go in that thing. It looks like something he salvaged from his scrap yard."

Aidan insisted that it was safe, so away they went. Aidan sat upfront with Louie, and Whitney was crammed behind the pilot's seat, like a sardine. It was a jump seat that folded down for maybe a child. She had a seat-belt and she was thankful for that restraint, because there wasn't a door on the right side of the single-engine plane.

It was late-summer, warm with clear skies and little to no wind. The plane's engine revved at the end of the runway and Louie lifted it off with ease. They flew low over the countryside with the perfect rows of golden corn fields. They were low enough to see the corn cobs so heavy their tips were dropping, showing signs of being ripe. Louie didn't have an IFR license, so he pretty much flew by the seat of his pants, as pilots would say. Aidan and Louie were chatting away up front, while Whitney was just hanging on and wondering if this would be her last flying adventure. Surprisingly, they landed smoothly and Louie dropped them off at the Minneapolis terminal and then he headed back to Grand Forks.

That was the last time they were in that overheating Cessna. Aidan traded or sold it and purchased a different

What Ever Happened to Whitney Lake?

Cessna with more powerful engines. The new plane was also pressurized so no masks were needed when they flew at higher altitudes. Whitney was more than happy that that airplane was gone. She was sure that her life had been extended for a few more years without the Cessna. In fact, she told Aidan that she wasn't going to fly with him anymore if he insisted on piloting that plane. He just shrugged his shoulders, but didn't comment. He supposed she wasn't serious, but this time, she was.

Some months later, Aidan was told that the person who had purchased the over-heating Cessna had crashed and died somewhere out west in the Rocky Mountains. Aidan appeared sorry, and said he should have scrapped it rather than sell it to another foolish pilot who thought he could make it work.

Chapter 8

The whirlwind continued with skiing in the famous Portillo Chile. This is where Mr. Portilla was returning from when he was a passenger on one of Whitney's flights from Miami that July two years prior. The ski area had been constructed in the 1940s and had hosted the World Ski Championships in August of 1966. The mountains were mostly treeless, with jagged grey and mostly black rocks, and little sign of any life. Whitney did see a Condor gliding above the valley, and at first, she thought it was an airplane, until its wings began to slowly flap. The giant bird has a wingspan of over ten feet. Somewhere in the sharp peaks of the Andes, the countries of Chile and Argentina meld together. The highest mountains along the boundaries of the two countries are just shy of 23,000 feet, and Whitney doubted if anyone had ventured across this unforbidden landscape. The ski season was usually mid-June to early October. This challenging area had become one of the key areas for training of the downhill racers worldwide.

Aidan and Whitney boarded a small bus in Santiago and bounced along the rough and narrow streets for more than an hour. They arrived at the cog-train station close to 10:00 am, and boarded the train, seated in one of the dining cars along with the other passengers. The idea was to have a leisurely lunch as the train's noisy cogs grabbed and edged its way up the steep mountain. The only road was similar to a logging trail, and had limited use for bringing skiers up the mountain, as well as supplies to service the hotel. The trail was often not passable in the winter because of avalanches, and the local maintenance didn't have any adequate equipment to clear away the heavy snow.

Shortly after they finished their lunch, the train pulled into the Portillo station, which was really just a platform to allow the passengers to unload their luggage. The hotel picked up all the bags and ski equipment and brought it to the hotel for the guests to claim. The lone resort hotel that nestled between the jagged landscape found many gasping for air with just a short walk from the train to the hotel. All the passengers had come from sea level and the altitude was almost 9,500 feet at the base of the ski area. In late afternoon, the train would head back down the mountain. Some sightseers would take the train up in the morning, have lunch at the hotel, and board the afternoon train to return to Santiago.

They were told that it was not unusual for storms to drop snow up to five feet in a day or so, and the train

What Ever Happened to Whitney Lake?

would have to wait for the tracks to be cleared. They were also informed, that it was not uncommon for guests to be stranded for a few extra days. That was a heads-up for Whitney, because she needed to be in contact with the airlines, and didn't want to be stranded in the Andes. The hotel assured her that they keep a close eye on the weather, and if it looked like a big storm was coming, that they should be able to get back down the mountain before the storm engulfed the area.

~

The stately hotel looked comfortable, with most rooms having a view of the ski mountain or the lagoon and the valley where the resort was built. The hotel provided all the services for their week's visit. The train climbed up the mountain twice a week with guests but also all the hotel's supplies.

Angie Koenig Olson

The view was breathtakingly beautiful, with an amphitheater of mountains with jagged peaks seeming to fall into the open water at the base of the hotel.

The first morning of skiing was met with a bit of a surprise, with many signs that said: **Danger, Hazardous Ice.** The wind that whipped across the open ski-slopes, was relentless, turning a fresh snow into a sheet of ice within a matter of hours. Whitney was told that the ski patrol was trained to stop a fallen skier from sliding into the rock wall at the hotel, or into the lagoon, or other unknown dangers. The terrain was so slick and steep, that if a skier fell, there was little chance of recovering without help.

On their first day of skiing, Whitney watched a ski patrol lie down in front of a fallen skier, as he dug into the icy slope. Both the skier and the patrol were both entangled while sliding down the slope, but at least at a slower pace.

The chairlift was often stopped as the wind became too hazardous to continue. One time, Whitney and Aidan were dangling high above the slopes when the wind was blowing so hard that it whipped a chair off the cable right in front of them. They watched the chair fly through the air and slide down the steep terrain for a few hundred

What Ever Happened to Whitney Lake?

feet. The chair finally stopped, cradled in a precipitous ravine below. It appeared that only the weight of their bodies being on the chair kept the pulley on the cable. Whitney was hoping that their chair had some sort of a lock to the cable, but she doubted it.

The chairs would rattle and squeak around the turn style, and at times, it was almost comical as the chair lift would stop and get hung up as it made the turn to let skiers' board. A workman would climb up the side of the idle chair, give the pulley a few good whacks with a hammer, and the chair lift was back to working again. It was indeed a very simple solution to the problem, and brought a smile to Whitney's face.

Whitney didn't recall ever seeing any snow-grooming equipment anywhere in Chile. At Portillo, she saw the Chilean Army sidestepping the steep terrain in hopes of packing the snow for the visitors. The men were also hoping to deter the avalanches from devastating the ski runs. Every now and then they would see a soldier lose his footing and topple head over heels to the bottom of the steep mountain side. The soldiers didn't have normal skis, but rather a board with a leather strap that was wrapped around their boots. It just seemed like it was part of another day in the high Andes Mountains.

The skiing at Portillo was extremely steep and icy, and Whitney often wondered why Aidan liked to ski there so much. It must have been to explore the different parts of the world and brush elbows with the contrasting cultures. He wasn't very good at the sport and often complained about the conditions, while Whitney was usually able to adjust to whatever was before her.

Still, it was a beautiful week with perfect weather during the day and crisp star-lit nights. In the evenings, the dining room was dimly lit with Andean musicians playing softly in the background. They drank pisco sours and dreamingly slow danced across the wooden floor, not even noticing if anyone else was there. Those were the times when Whitney was sure she wanted to continue to be with Aidan, wherever the adventures would take them.

~

On one of their ski trips to South America, Aidan and Whitney skied at an area outside of Santiago that you could drive to for day skiing. As the ten-passenger van crawled up the steep road to La Parva and Farellones, a little more than 30 miles from Santiago, Whitney noticed signs along the way that said, "CAUTION, ONE WAY." The road was designated as up in the morning and down after 12 noon. There were only small turnouts at some of the sharp switchbacks and no guard-rails along the steep drop-offs. Not everyone paid attention to the road rules, and more than once, their van was dangling over an edge as a speeding vehicle met them head-on with no care about going the wrong way. More than two hours later, they finally arrived at Farellones. Whitney had been gripping whatever she could find to hang onto in the van for the entire trip, and she could finally take a deep breath again.

Whitney looked at Aidan and said, "I won't take that trip up again. We will have to stay at the ski area, or only ski for the day. That road is a death wish."

Aidan looked at her in amazement and a little confused, but agreed to find a place to stay if they wanted to spend another day at Farellones. La Parva was just a few miles down the mountain, but they were told that there wasn't a place to stay there. All of the dwellings were privately owned and not available to rent.

They purchased day tickets at a small structure at Farellones that served simple food and had a few rental rooms in the back. They headed out into the intense sunshine and a beautiful day of relatively easy skiing. The snow was soft and easy to carve, with a modest terrain, compared to the challenging Portillo. At the end of the day, they inquired about staying for a night or two. As it was, the only place to stay was the place where they purchased the ski-tickets and that was the same place they had a quite delicious Chilean-style lunch when they had first arrived. The lunch had consisted of a large bowl of steaming broth with swimming vegetables and a shank of some sort of meat, and freshly baked bread. Whitney had the feeling that all the meals were the same. The small inn had three rooms in the back, with a pot-belly stove in the hall outside the rooms. Each room had its own shower etc. Whitney said, "It looks like it will be OK for a few nights."

That evening the host lit an abundance of candles, and Whitney was thinking, *how romantic.* To her surprise, the power generator was turned off at 9pm, and the candles were their only light. After a full day of skiing a bed was more than welcome. There were two twin beds in their small room already piled high with heavy blankets. Stepping sideways, there was just room enough to slide between the two beds. Whitney found it to be quite chilly in their room, so she left her long-underwear on that she had on for skiing. She crawled in under the layers of covers, and fell asleep, not thinking too much about the cold room.

In the morning, there was no water in the tap, and a thin coat of ice on the bathroom floor. Whitney guessed that the water pipes had broken during the night. They somehow survived the night with the mountain of blankets on each bed. They slipped their ski clothes back on, and made their way to the tables in front of the humble-abode for breakfast. Aidan and Whitney agreed that they couldn't stay another night without heat. Aidan also added that he had slipped on the ice on the bathroom floor. The ticket seller behind the desk looked at them with surprise, with little to no concern if Aidan was injured. He just ignored the comment and said he would fire-up the pot-belly stove later in the day. The mountains were almost treeless, so wood was scarce and coal would be the next choice for the heater. Aidan piped up and said, "We will pay more for heat." The man behind the desk gave Aidan a small smile and a nod as Aidan slipped a wad of pesos in his hand.

They stayed three nights in total, with wonderful skiing. The food was all served in a bowl with the unfamiliar meat, usually with a big bone, a few vegetables that were floating around in a golden broth, and served with a basket of home-made biscuits. They were not sure what they were eating, but it was always good after a full day of skiing.

They only lasted three days at Farellones, mostly because they weren't able to shower for any of the days that they were there. The water pipes had indeed burst, as they had thought, and the plumber wouldn't be up the mountain for a few more days. As it was, all they had to wash with was a pitcher of water and a pan from the kitchen. At that point, all Whitney could think about was a nice hot shower back in Santiago.

The dusty van that originally brought the tourists up the mountain, arrived just before noon. The tired-looking driver loaded their bags and ski equipment up on the roof of the van and they headed back down to Santiago. About half way down the mountain, Whitney looked over at Aidan as the van was swaying back and forth around the hairpin curves. Aidan seemed to be in deep thought and didn't seem to notice the rough road. Suddenly, he came out of his trance and looked over at Whitney and said, "Why don't we catch a flight across the Andes to Buenos Aires. There is a ski area south of there that I would like to see. It is actually in Patagonia. They call it, Tirerra del Fuego. The land of fire. The locals say it is the end of the world. It also has a very interesting history."

Apparently Aidan had not had enough skiing yet. As it was, they had planned to go to Portillo on that trip but the ski-racing teams from around the world were practicing, and the mountain was closed to visitors. It was interesting that Aidan had not checked in advance to see if Portillo was available for tourists.

Whitney was thinking to herself and finally said aloud, "Patagonia sounds so intriguing. The end of the world, as the locals said. I'm all for going there!"

Chapter 9

Whitney was fortunate to have such flexible employment. If she wanted to go on an extended trip with Aidan, she could easily take a leave of absence, or give her flights away to other stewardesses. The company was generously staffed at the time, and welcomed employees taking time off for personal reasons. During one of their South American jaunts, two of the NWA unions were on strike, so there wasn't a reason to hurry back to the states. She didn't have a date that she would have to be back to work, so she'd check every few days with a local airline in South America to see if the NWA strike was settled. NWA said that she would have a few days advance notice as to when she would have to return to work. So, she and Aidan just kept traveling.

When Aidan asked Whitney if she would like to go to Argentina, she was quite obviously excited. It seemed like a destination that no one else had ever ventured to, at least no one that she knew.

As it turned out, it wasn't easy to book a flight from Santiago Chile to Buenos Aires Argentina. There was only one flight a day between the two countries, and the fierce winds across the Andes often caused flights to be canceled; sometimes for a few days. Aidan would check with the airline in the morning, and if the flight was canceled, they'd spend the time touring around Chile's countryside. On one of their grounded days, they hired a car to take them down to the beach and a seaside restaurant for a late afternoon lunch. The drive was breathtaking as the taxi hugged the road's sharp curves and switch-backs while craggy-black volcanic rock formations jetted out all along the bluffs. The whole scene was juxtaposed against endless falls of colorful lush gardens spilling down over the bluffs. Whitney thought this must be like the hanging gardens of Babylon. Private homes, hotels and services were all nestled into the rocks just before the land seemed to fall away into the ocean.

They ate of the fresh catch of delicious fish for lunch on a grand hotel veranda, with the sounds of the sea crashing against the rocks below.

What Ever Happened to Whitney Lake?

The landscape all around Chile is young and wild, and earthquakes and a rumbling volcano are a fairly common occurrence. There are well over 100 active volcanos in Chile, and the locals are not surprised when the earth shakes. Most of the population is nestled along the rough and rugged shoreline, where the residents enjoy a fairly mild climate year around.

~

It was three days later, when the winds calmed enough to travel over the Andes and on to Buenos Aires. When the tops of the mountains are over 22,000 feet, it seemed so strange to be flying so close to the jagged peaks.

Angie Koenig Olson

They spent a few days in Buenos Aires, finding it to be the Paris of South America, with famous designer showrooms at almost every street corner, and high-styled men and women sauntering on the streets like fashion models, and maybe they were. Whitney had to admit, she was feeling a little out-of-style walking among the locals, and she had to make use of her one little black dress that she had packed. Aidan insisted on buying her some of Argentina's famous soft leathers that included a white leather coat and a pink skirt and jacket. Although she thought the leathers were exceptional, she didn't see any ladies wearing leather on the street. *Odd,* she thought. *Maybe it is just for the tourists.*

~

From Buenos Aires, they finally boarded the plane to Bariloche in the Patagonia region of Argentina. At the time, there was only one flight a week that came to this out-of-the-way destination. When they purchased their flight ticket, they were told that they needed to arrange transportation from where the plane landed to go up to the ski resort.

~

The twin engine Boeing jet landed softly on the single strip in the desert, with only a small building that resembled a skating warming-house. What little vegetation there was, was brown or dormant and with little to no signs of life, animal or human. But, it was winter there. Nobody lived at the landing strip and only when a flight was scheduled was there anyone around for miles. There were no ground services that could be seen anywhere. They climbed down the aircraft stairs and waited a few minutes. Aidan and Whitney realized that one of them had to crawl into the aircraft belly and retrieve their luggage. Aidan hoisted himself up into the aircraft belly, and handed the bags down to Whitney. They seemed to be the only passengers with luggage. Everyone else just hopped off the plane and into a waiting car with maybe a briefcase and/or an overnight bag. Aidan and Whitney, on the other hand had been traveling for over two weeks by now, and not only had travel bags, but all their ski equipment.

Fortunately, the car they ordered, was waiting, and the driver loaded their bags and skis and they headed up the mountain. Aidan and Whitney looked around as they were leaving the landing strip and it was like the twilight zone. The aircraft looked like it had been abandoned in the desert, in the middle of nowhere. There was not a person to be seen in any direction. Whitney thought that it seemed surreal to think that they were going to snow-ski here, when there was nothing but wasteland with small mountains peaking up to the north on the distant horizon. It truly felt like Tierra del Fuego, the end of the world, as the locals would say; the gateway to Antarctica.

But they weren't deceived; once they left the desert, the scenery quickly changed to skirting around a fairly large deep glacial lake called Nahuel Huapi. The water was a deep azure-blue and appeared bottomless and unforgiving. As quickly as their car passed the lake, it skirted the city of Bariloche and began climbing up the narrowing road, until suddenly tall pine trees blocked the view of the city and any landscape beyond the road. Whitney opened her car-window and inhaled deeply, as the heavenly aroma of the conifers drifted inside the car. It was about a half-hour drive up to the ski area. She was quite surprised to see the grand hotel at the end of their drive, and it certainly was in the middle of nowhere.

It was well-known to the people in South America. As history recorded, the Germans had built this lavish resort in the 1930s. And later, when the Nazi Germans needed to escape Europe, they mostly traveled by waiting ships out of the southern tip of Italy, and already had all the arrangements made for a life in many of the eastern countries in South America after WWII. This was one of the safe places in the world for the uprooted Germans. The entire Bariloche area is mired in Nazi lore, some of it true although some could be fallacious.

What Ever Happened to Whitney Lake?

Cerro Catedral Alta Patagonia was the official name of the ski resort. When Aidan and Whitney visited in the late 1960s, it was about the size of a small mid-west hill, with a ski run on each side of the toe. It was a chain-toe, not a rope-toe that you clamped onto to ride up the ski hill. The chain rattled and scraped continuously as it slid up and down the hill from early morning until the hill closed in late afternoon.

An attendant at the bottom of the hill, collected pesos equivalent to 25cents. He proceeded to wrap a wide leather belt around Whitney's waist, and told her to grab the chain with the meat-hook that was dangling on a chain that hung on the leather belt. The attendant placed the hook in Whitney's hand, and she was on her own. After clamping on, she was wondering how it would release at the top of the hill. As it was, she landed on a flat area and was easily able to release the enchainment. At the top of the hill, an attendant removed the belt from Whitney's waist and she was free to ski down the rather short and easy slope. From then on, each time she went back up, the ritual repeated, with paying for the belt, etc., etc. The snow was soft and the temperature was mild with sunny skies and an altitude of about 6,800 feet. The trip to Bariloche was certainly for the adventure, not for the greatest skiing in the world.

The hotel was classic German architecture, with dark mahogany wood and dim lighting. Aidan and Whitney had the same waiter, at the same table, for every meal in the dining room. The server wore the same soiled sort-of-white apron day after day, and hovered over them as if they were going to disappear and he would have no one to serve. They socialized with people from Paraguay and Uruguay and wondered if they were some of Hitler's escapees after WWII. Aidan didn't ask if they were from Europe, but they looked to be Northern European and spoke English with a German accent. Although Portuguese is the language of eastern South America, (on the western side it is Spanish) they could hear many different European languages spoken.

In all their travels to any of the South American countries they were met with people very interested in the American visitors. Very few Americans ventured to this remote part of the world. They weren't as interested in them so much as they were interested in purchasing their American ski equipment. A limited selection of equipment was manufactured in South America at that time, and the locals said that the quality was poor compared to the American equipment. So, when they saw a pair of Rosemount boots and Head skis, strangers were quick to ask if they would be willing to sell any of their equipment; skis, boots, poles, and even clothing. So, that is what Aidan and Whitney did; they sold for the dollars they paid in the United States, and had thus less to transport home. Most of the locals carried a roll of American dollars, and were delighted to spend the dollars on the equipment.

The next morning, they watched the tall handsome young man from Paraguay stroll through the hotel lobby sporting Aiden's ski coat, pants (a little short) and the Rosemount boots. He was delighted but Whitney doubted if he was very comfortable; he looked as if he was in pain. He was very gracious and handed Whitney a package that she thought was a thank you, but later realized was just a customary gift gesture when they enjoyed meeting someone. The package contained a white angora sweater with aqua birds in flight across the front. The tag said that it was handmade in Argentina.

She really didn't know how to thank him for what she thought was an extravagant gift from a stranger. It was just a shrug of his shoulders, as the tall stranger said, "It is really nothing, just a small memento from South America."

Whitney smiled and reached for his hand and said, "Thank you." She was lost for any more words.

Later that day, Whitney and Aidan boarded the weekly flight from The Patagonia region back to Buenos Ares, and eventually they would fly on to Rio De Janeiro.

For years, Whitney kept the sweater, mostly just to remind her of the kind gesture in this unusual happenstance in a foreign land.

Chapter 10

Once again, Whitney found herself being a little self-conscious mingling with the stylish dressed men and women in Argentina. Most of the ladies were in mid-calf, torso-hugging dresses, and at least three-inch high-heals. The men were in black or grey suits or sport-coats, and most times a bright colored necktie and a stiffly starched, bright-white shirt. The locals seemed to have a lot of idol time to just sit or stand around and chat to each other, or to just be people watching. No one seemed to be in a hurry.

They stayed in Buenos Ares for just two days, enjoying the high-style and unhurried motion of the streets. They strolled through an outdoor market place and purchased silk scarfs for just a few dollars, and ate at a nearby outdoor café, observing the strollers who seemed like models parading down the promenade.

~

They left Buenos Aires and landed next in Rio De Janeiro where they checked into the Copacabana Palace Hotel, across the busy thoroughfare from the Copacabana

Beach. Being winter there, the famous beach was void of sunbathers, but hundreds of kites were flying high in the restless wind that comes down from the mountains to the east. The constant, but choppy breeze gave life to the kites that zoomed up and down the expanse of sand and around the rocks that jut up out of the bay.

In the evening, the hotel offered a sleek dance floor and live entertainment. The Latin samba or rumba seemed to echo everywhere in the hotel or on the streets of Rio. Aidan ventured out on the dance floor as Whitney tried to show him the steps in the samba. He seemed eager, but they needed more time to practice. Whitney was sure that he hadn't danced much before in his life, while Whitney felt at home dancing anywhere in the world. She sensed that she had brought something to Aidan's life that he hadn't really enjoyed before. Most of the hotels that they stayed at had dance floors, and Whitney was the first to glide onto the floor, no matter what music was playing.

As part of the evening entertainment, they were fortunate to see Carman Miranda dancing the samba with a bunch of fruit strapped to her head. Whitney had only seen pictures of this in the USA and thought maybe it wasn't for real, but it was. There Carman was, as stiff as a mummy, trying to keep the fruit balanced on her head while dancing a samba.

What Ever Happened to Whitney Lake?

They stepped outside the hotel to find Rio wonderfully alive at night, with Latin music spilling out onto the streets from every hotel or club. People carried brightly colored fabrics that floated above them, seemingly keeping in time to the music. The music was strangely soothing and exciting to Whitney, as she and Aidan strolled hand-in-hand along the busy avenue, forgetting that the rest of the world existed.

The next morning, they decided to have breakfast at the pool at the Copacabana hotel. Although it was winter, it was still warm enough to sit outside and enjoy the warm sunshine. Aidan said he would order breakfast in Spanish, and they ended up with a tray full of vegetables. They both laughed about that, and said they needed to purchase a Spanish book, but Whitney doubted if that would ever happen.

Most of the tables were occupied by men (who appeared to be mostly Germans) apparently doing business, with a bottle of bourbon or whisky propped in the middle of their tables. Liquor appeared center stage for every meal in the Latin countries. Whitney was thinking what a high tolerance they must have for alcohol, to be drinking so early in the day.

~

Rio was filled with the extremely wealthy who occupied the beachfront and bedded at the lavish hotels.

After breakfast, Aidan and Whitney walked further into the city and discovered how extreme life is away from the Copacabana.

The back streets were littered with beggars and the sick, often sitting or lying down on the concrete, or propped up by a street light pole or their own box or cart that had become their home. These were the people who weren't fortunate enough to live at the Favela.

"Where is that place, the Favela?" asked Whitney.

Aidan said, "The Favela is the slum on Rio's hillsides. If you look up and to the north from the beach, you can catch a glimpse from a distance."

Once Whitney knew where to look, it became so obvious as to what she was seeing.

What Ever Happened to Whitney Lake?

For miles, as far as Whitney could see, burrowed into the mountainside were the lean-to shacks of the shantytown, or what the locals called the Favela. Aidan convinced a reluctant cab driver to take them up to see this forbidden place. He stuffed some bills into the cabbie's hand as the driver hesitated, then he looked up and said that he would take them, but he also said that he wasn't allowed to drive his taxi inside the Favela or he would be fired. The fringe would certainly be close enough for Whitney. She wasn't sure how safe it was, but when they started driving to the edge of the area, she could already smell the stench of the open sewers. The people who lived there didn't want any strangers looking at them and would quickly turn their backs, as if they were hiding. Their life in the Favela seemed so hopeless. She wondered, if anyone was ever able to leave the slum and have a better life. Somehow, it seemed so out-of-reach for the people born into that wretched, forbidden place.

The inhabitants of shantytown, scrounged for just about everything they had. Most of the shanties were built from stolen materials, and/or whatever they could find unsecured by an inattentive owner. The cabby said that one could see them scavenging through the trash at construction sites or in back-alleys during the dark hours. He also said that the restaurants didn't always throw the left-over food in the trash, but left it outside the back door for the poor.

~

After being to the Favela, Whitney needed someplace to settle her nerves. It didn't seem to affect Aidan—she assumed he had seen poverty like this many times in his travels. She left Aidan back at the hotel and walked across the busy street from the Copacabana Palace Hotel to the miles of seemingly endless sandy beach. She wanted to see if she could see the shantytown from the beach, and she could, off in a distance, now that she knew what to look for.

What Ever Happened to Whitney Lake?

She stood amidst the hundreds of huge, colorful kites flying above her. There were kites of airplanes and kites of birds and exotic and make-believe animals. She found herself spinning around on the sand with her arms spread out and her face to the sky, in this strange world of make-believe. She felt the tension ease inside her as she thought about how the kites echoed the bright colors of the shanties, while the kites lazily swayed back and forth in the ocean breeze. At least the poor seemed to have an abundance of color in their lives.

For weeks after visiting the Favela, Whitney could still bring back the helpless pictures of the people, and the smell, that pungent smell, of the open sewers that constantly trickled down the hillside.

~

By the time they decided that the South American adventure was over, Whitney was called back to work and was honestly glad to be going home. They had been tromping around South America for more than three weeks. Aidan never seemed to be in a hurry to return home. His business seemed to run itself while he was traipsing around, with what seemed like not a care in the world.

Whitney still liked to think that she had a life separate from Aidan, and looked forward to returning to the United States. She also looked forward to getting back to work and to her flying-friends. She didn't think that Aidan understood her need to want a life separate from him. He certainly thought that his life was as good as it gets, and in some ways it was, but not for Whitney, not now anyway.

Chapter 11

In early winter that same year, Aidan suggested a tour of Europe. He had business in Scotland, and from there, they would take-in the culture of the different countries and visit the many museums and churches in England, France, Italy, and Belgium, and finish the trip with skiing in Switzerland.

Whitney took a leave of absence for three weeks. Although she really was looking forward to spending time at her newly-purchased home, Aidan seemed to plan the perfect trips so that she wouldn't say no.

They landed at Heathrow Airport in London, and boarded a train to Scotland. Along the way, they sat in a car facing another business-man. Aidan said, "Watch this. The British won't ever speak to a stranger first, but once you say a word or two to them, you can't button them up." And it was true. The nicely suited man was buried in his newspaper, but as soon as Aidan asked the man where he was headed, the conversation went on from there, with the Brit folding his paper and chattering all the way to Dundee.

The train rumbled over numerous bridges, with spectacular views of the many lochs in Scotland. Some time back the glaciers had slowly carved deep ravines and swallowed up the land as the masses of ice moved on along their downward course. It was a dramatic but forbidding landscape with little to no sign of life except an occasional abandoned medieval castle.

It was almost nine hours later when the train pulled into the Dundee station, and the Englishman's chatter finally ended. Whitney had never seen Aidan talk so much. Whitney's ears were ringing from the clatter of the train and the rattle of the Englishman.

What Ever Happened to Whitney Lake?

Whitney stayed back at the Hotel Dundee while Aidan left for his business. She never knew where he went or who he was meeting. In some ways, she didn't really care, and yet he was always so mysterious about where he ventured off to. Whitney found Dundee to be cold, damp and colorless, with the stone buildings stained black from burning coal. She was glad to leave and return to England and on to the mainland.

~

Aidan said, "If we do nothing else in London, we have to go to Hyde Park on Sunday. You will see flamboyant and impromptu orators get up on a soapbox and express their opinions on politics, religion, or any subject they choose. As long as the person is on the soapbox, they can say whatever comes to mind. They are known as the Sunday Soapbox Orators."

By the time they arrived at the park, midday on Sunday, voices were piercing the air seemingly coming from all directions. Politics seemed to dominate, but there were many opinions about the Queen and all the British royalty. It was rare to hear a positive voice, most were against the laws and lack of freedom.

Whitney found this very intriguing, and listened to at least three different attention-getters. There looked to be close to a dozen speakers scattered around the park.

What Ever Happened to Whitney Lake?

She was told that this Sunday ritual had been going on since 1872, and was never lacking for speakers. Each one had to bring their own soapbox, or it could be a chair or anything that would lift them above the potential crowd.

Whitney left London thinking, *Aidan was right about going to Hyde Park.* She would never forget it.

~

Being winter in Europe, it seemed cold and damp in all the hotels and in any of the heatless buildings. Whitney quickly came to realize why there was a hot-water bottle warming her bed back in London. At first she thought it was just a really nice gesture, but soon realized that none of the old stone hotels had a central heating system.

In Italy, when they checked in at the hotel front desk, the clerk took both their passports, looked at Whitney's, then at Aidan's, with a question mark on her face.

When they took the elevator up three floors to their room, Aidan mentioned that she should not be surprised if she was pinched in the butt. He said, "The Italian men pinch ladies if they approve of you." Sure enough, Whitney was pinched, but it still came as a surprise.

They left the hotel two days later, with the same clerk working at the front desk. She asked Aidan if his daughter had a nice stay in Rome. Whitney knew Aidan was very uncomfortable with this question, as his face flushed a little. He nodded to the clerk and quickly took Whitney's arm and said, "Let's go."

~

They visited many of the great cathedrals and viewed the Mona Lisa at the Louvre Museum in France. Whitney was awestruck by all the history, beauty and talent that was right in front of her. South America had had such a different flavor than what she was experiencing in Europe.

In contrast to all the art and history, Aidan wanted to go the Folies Bergère in Paris. It would be Whitney's first experience with topless girls sauntering across the stage. It was hard for her to remember their costumes, there was so little fabric. Aidan would look at her occasionally and smile to see what her reaction was. She was trying to be sophisticated enough to at least appear to be enjoying the show. She was surprised at Aidan, who was showing no emotion about the topless girls, and thinking that Whitney would like this topless theater. Whitney only remembered the ostrich feathers swaying from one side of the stage to another. All the girls did is parade around. Their strolling beauty was apparently their talent.

In the wee hours of the morning, they climbed the stairs of a quaint old house where the famous Lescargot Montorgueil restaurant was perched above the Paris market. They ate the delicate escargot that was swimming in garlic butter, while men below carried half a cow or pig strung across their back. The animal carcasses were loaded into waiting trucks that would make their way to the local restaurants before dawn. This was the famous restaurant from the film. "Irma La Douce." And, it was Whitney's first escargot. Whitney wondered how many times that Aidan had been to this charming place and what other girl had hung onto his arm? He seemed to know exactly where to go and what to do everywhere they ventured.

~

After a couple of weeks of visiting art galleries, churches and even the Vatican in Rome, it was time to head to Switzerland. They landed in Zurich, and boarded a train that puffed its way up the mountain for more than three hours from an altitude of 408 meters to 1,560 meters. Devos is known to be the highest town in all of Europe. This charming and grand resort town of Devos sits at the base of the Matterhorn Mountain.

There were local taxis waiting at the train station but Aidan chose to take a horse-drawn carriage to the Tschuggen Grand Hotel. The 1883 hotel had 98 rooms and was built over a natural hot spring. The immense hot spring pool was outdoor and indoor, with steam billowing outside in the cool mountain air.

As they were checking in at the lobby, Whitney looked around at the other hotel guests to see if there were any Americans or if they were mostly Europeans. She was right, it appeared that they were the only Americans.

It quickly became quite obvious to her that none of the women who stayed at this hotel skied but spent the day primping for the evening dinner and dancing.

What Ever Happened to Whitney Lake?

Late afternoon on the first day, Aidan and Whitney strolled hand in hand, up and down the snow-packed walkways of Devos, glancing in shop windows and noticing a pair of goat-fur boots. They stepped inside the store and each tried on a pair of these funky boots and walked out of the store donning their new purchase. As they lingered along the avenue, passersby pointed and smiled or laughed at the two of them with goat feet.

That evening, Whitney went to the ladies' side of the spa, wearing her new boots. As she was changing into her swimsuit inside a small stall with an open bottom, a lady walked by and bent down to look at the floor where Whitney was changing and said, "Is there a dog in there? No dogs are allowed in the spa." Whitney laughed to herself and wanted to belt back and say, "No, there are two dogs." But, she didn't.

Angie Koenig Olson

~

On the first morning of skiing, the mountain was in the clouds. The trails were marked for the skiers to follow, until you could get to an open run. Aidan and Whitney skied from one yellow flag to another that marked the trail, until they were down the mountain far enough to be below the clouds. The snow was soft and easy to carve, and other than the mountain top staying in the clouds all day, it was uneventful.

The next day, the sun was brightly shining, as Whitney looked over the cliffs that they had skied by the day before, with a sense of uneasiness. Most skiing in countries other than the US, seemed to be *at your own risk*. The yellow flags that they followed they thought were suggestions, were actually a warning of dangerous drop-offs to either side of the trail.

~

That evening, when they entered the elegant restaurant, it appeared that they were on display when so many heads turned in their direction. The entrance was at the top, with seating that stepped down several levels. Whitney didn't care, she was here to ski and to enjoy the mountain town of Devos. She was glad that Aidan didn't care either but seemed to be amused by the stares. She ran her hands down the sides of her one black dress to straighten out any wrinkles as the maître d motioned for them to follow him. They stepped down several sets of steps and were seated in one of the booths for two. It seemed as if the other diners needed to keep glancing at them. Whitney's face was red and tan with pale goggle circles around her eyes. Some guests just looked and looked away, while others shook their head, wondering what the ordinary Americans were doing here.

~

On their last day at Devos, Whitney said, "Let's take the longest run down the mountain. It is a 12km run that will take us from Weissfluh Peak to Kueblis, and then we can take the train back up to Devos." Aidan agreed that it sounded interesting, and he really liked the milder skiing.

As it turned out, it was a very easy beginners' run with even rest stops and warming huts along the way. They started down the mountain under a cloudless sky. It was to be a perfect run and a perfect way to end the day. Unbeknownst to them was the condition of the lower part of the run. About two thirds of the way down, the snow dwindled quickly, and soon diminished to grass and mud. They walked the rest of the way down to the train station, slipping and sliding in their stiff ski boots. Aidan decided to take a shortcut through a farmer's pasture while Whitney stayed on the trail. The shortcut found him slipping on some animal dung and landing on his side, with the manure greased across his jacket, pants and boots. No doubt about it, he smelled like a farmyard. About an hour later, when they finally arrived at the station, they realized they couldn't board the train with him smelling as he did. Whitney found a water hose on the side of the train station and told Aidan that she needed to hose him down. "We absolutely have to get some of the brown matter stink off of you before we can board the train." She had the hose going full pressure and sprayed Aidan until he was too cold to continue. They stood on the platform away from other passengers, with Aidan's whole body shaking, even his teeth were chattering. The train finally arrived about a half hour later, and they waited to be the last to board.

When they finally boarded the crowded train, they found it filled with well-dressed ladies and gentlemen in business suits. It looked as if there was nowhere to go or to hide. There weren't any vacant seats, so they decided to stand in the back of the train-car, as far away from other passengers as possible. Heads still turned with noses sniffing to see where the putrid smell was coming from. Most of the passengers covered their faces in hopes that the smell would just go away. The half-hour ride seemed like the longest ride of Whitney's life, and once they exited the train they would still have to face the highbrows at the hotel.

They couldn't take a taxi or a carriage with Aidan's condition, so they walked back to the hotel the few blocks in their clumsy ski boots.

The doorman offered to get Aidan a clean robe from the hotel spa. He said they wouldn't be able to go up to their room in his condition. The doorman said, "I'll take care of your clothes." Whitney was sure that he was just going to drop them into the rubbish-bin. Aidan stepped behind the doorman's podium and slipped off his clothes down to his underwear. The doorman quickly snatched up the smelly pile and disappeared. Then Aidan said, "Oh well, it was worth it, no wonder we were the only skiers on that long trail. We were lucky to end up at the train station."

They left Devos without a further thought about Aidan's ski boots and clothes. He'd just purchase new in America.

~

Whitney was filled with volumes of great and interesting memories from all the different countries they had roamed.

But Whitney was ready to return to America and to her work with the airline. Aidan, on the other hand, seemed as if he could travel forever, with little thought of America being his home.

Chapter 12

It was early July, when Aidan said it was time to head to Florida for the annual Tarpon fishing. There is about a two-week window when schools of these lively fish stop to feed in the warm Florida waters. Whitney was excited to go ocean fishing, and Aidan said this was not like any other fishing in the world. Whitney wasn't sure if he was testing her or spoiling her with another rather exotic experience.

Aidan piloted the Cessna to Tampa where they rented a car and drove to the sleepy town of Boca Grande on Gasparilla Island. They stayed at a simple fisherman's motel, and Aidan asked, "Is the Pink Elephant Restaurant still in business.?

The motel owner said, " It sure is. Best place on the island for the catch of the day, maybe red snapper." Aidan said, "Great, we'll go there for red snapper tonight."

Whitney noticed a rather smirky-smile on Aidan's face, and wondered what that was about?

As it turned out, the restaurant was as sleepy as the island itself, with hurricane plywood leaning against the outside walls, just in case a storm was coming towards the island. There were just a few tables with red-checked tablecloths, and an air conditioner mounted high on the side-wall, blowing ice-cold-air, mostly to the ceiling, with just a little cooler air coming down to their table. The few windows in the front were covered in steam. Everything and everyone seemed to move in slow-motion in the heat. The owner sauntered over to their table, and greeted them with, "It's just another hot and steamy day in Boca Grande." His round face had beads of sweat running down his side-burns. His straggly hair was messy, as if he had just come from a nap. His appearance brought a smile to Aidan's face.

Aidan asked, "Do you have red snapper tonight?" The owner looked away and was somewhat apologetic that they hadn't made it out to the wreck that day, which is where they line-catch the snapper. Aidan looked at Whitney and chuckled, and said, "For as many years that I have been coming here, they have never made it out to the wreck that day." They ordered the fish of the day, and whatever it was, it was fresh and delicious.

Whitney wondered why they called the restaurant the Pink Elephant. Maybe it was because Ringling Brothers wintered the circus animals in Sarasota, not all that far away from Boca Grande. Seemed like a likely reason to Whitney, but the restaurant owner just shrugged his shoulders without an answer. Maybe it was just too hot for his brain to remember.

As they strolled back to the motel after dinner, Whitney could feel the sweat dripping through her hair and down the side of her face. The sun was low on the horizon, but Whitney knew that the night offered only a slight relief from the heat. Aidan didn't seem to be bothered by the thick hot air, and moved along with little attention to anything but the exciting fishing early the next morning. Whitney was thinking how uncomfortable this sleepy island was day and night. She was not sure that she would want to stay more than a few days. The boat the next morning would be a welcome relief to her, with at least a bit of a breeze from its movement.

~

They lazily walked along the wharf just before sunset. The fishing boats were rocking in the water with the gentle roll of the ocean. The crimson sky was brilliant with the last rays of the sun sinking past the horizon. Aidan said, "Look out to the sea, you may see the tarpon rolling on the surface of the water. They travel in a school, sometimes called a shoal, and often can be seen at dusk and dawn. For just a few weeks in mid- summer, it is possible to see hundreds of tarpon traveling together to feed here in Florida's warm tropical waters."

Whitney didn't see any tarpon that evening, just the gentle roll of the ocean before being swallowed up by the moonless night.

Before dawn the next morning they were at the wharf and ready to board the charter boat for the early morning run. Later in the day, they would return again for the sunset fishing. Several charters were heading out to the open waters at the same time. The boat captain had the rods ready and the bait in a five-gallon bucket. "Hop aboard," the captain said, as he revved the engine and tossed the ropes to the dock.

They headed out to deeper waters and where the captain knew the tarpon would be feeding. Whitney was delighted with the cooling breeze rustling through her hair as the boat purred along. The sun began peeking out above the horizon when the boatman slowed the boat and said, "When you can see the tarpon, they won't hit on your bait. The fish are playing when they are on the surface." The boat was adrift bobbing around amidst sometimes hundreds of tarpon. They would surface and role and dive and repeat it for what seemed like hours, but it was actually maybe an hour or two. The fish couldn't have cared less that any of the boats were in their playground.

Then, the boatman said, "The waters will suddenly become still, and the tarpon will disappear; they are diving deep to feed. It is then time to let your line out, and wait for a hit."

It is truly sport fishing. The challenge is to see if the fish tires first or the fisherman. Mid-morning, Whitney had a hit and her line whizzed out of her reel in lightning speed. The captain said, "Keep the line tight, no matter if the tarpon swims deep or if it jumps in the air. They will often jump out of the water and dance on their tail to try to spit out the hook. Their mouth is all bone, so no slack in the line, or the hook is released."

Angie Koenig Olson

Whitney was lucky to land one tarpon on her first day of fishing, in about 25 minutes. She was not sure how much it weighed, but it was common to be between 60 and 150 pounds. When both fisherman and fish were exhausted, the tarpon was brought alongside the boat. The boatman brought the fish into the boat for a picture if wanted, and then he gently slid the fish back into the water. Whitney was amazed and delighted that she had actually boated a tarpon, and then had the pleasure of watching the tarpon ever so slowly swim away, both of them equally exhausted.

Aidan had been to these waters for tarpon many times, but Whitney thought she was the only girl who had been asked to come with him.

Aidan said, "We'll come back again next July, you seem to be a natural at this."

Whitney felt that that was true.

They dined at the Pink Elephant for the two evenings they were in Boca Grande and asked for the red snapper. Both nights, the squatty server thought briefly, then said, "No, they didn't make it out to the wreck today." It really didn't matter, all the fish was fresh and delicious, no matter what kind.

Whitney began to think that the Pink Elephant's catch-of-the-day and the red snapper had become something of a joke to the locals, and to anyone who came here for the tarpon fishing.

~

Before, during and after every trip they took together, Aidan would express his dislike for her working, and wanted her to quit flying. He would often degrade it as a menial job and said that he would take care of her in a proper way. That way, she would be free to travel with him whenever he wanted her to, rather than them having to plan around her work schedule.

Whitney felt she would have to make the decision around remaining a working girl, in which case possibly having to give up Aidan's lavish lifestyle. There were times when she just returned from a three or four-day work-trip, and he would be at her doorstep wanting to leave the next morning for another jaunt to Puerto Rico or Acapulco. It was hard to say no to some of his adventures, but she really wanted to spend some time at her new home and away from people for a few days.

As much as Whitney liked traveling with Aidan, she still liked her flying job. But, little by little, she knew that freedom was dwindling. There was no way she would ever be able to do the things she was doing on her own. Was she falling in-love with him? Or, was she in love with his life-style?

Part II

Taming Whitney

Chapter 13

As much as Whitney wanted to keep her independence, Aidan kept the pressure on for them to start a life together out of Minnesota and preferably the Colorado Mountains. Whitney knew her airline job had a limited life, and she had concerns about having to retire at 31, which was still a few years away, but constantly in the back of her mind. By now, Aidan had moved into an apartment in the city, and said he was officially separated from his estranged wife.

With some hesitation, Whitney finally conceded, and said she would quit the airline and go with him to the mountains and they would make a life there together. Aidan wanted a place where he could fly the Cessna in and out, possibly right on the ranch property. Again, it seemed very exotic and captivating to Whitney. Their life so far had certainly been that of a fairy tale in Whitney's eyes. From remote places in South America, to the Matterhorn in Switzerland, and all the unexpected destinations where they brushed elbows with celebrities and jetsetters around the world. It was a hard lifestyle to think about giving up, and would certainly be hard to forget. For almost three years, they bobbed in an out of countries, seemingly without a need to stop the whirlwind and to settle in one place. Many of their destinations Aidan had visited before and he wanted to show Whitney his favorites. And then there were the many other landing-places that were because of Aidan's apparently endless thirst for anything new, different or to some degree skirting the edge of danger.

~

They looked at homes in ski-areas, and ventured out to ranches in the Colorado mountain valleys. Whitney and Aidan had skied at a number of the resorts in the area, but were not sure that they wanted to live in a heavily populated mountain village. Both Whitney and Aidan seemed to want a little less people and more wide-open spaces.

~

Now that the decision was made to commit, Whitney felt compelled to tell Aidan about her childhood, and mostly about her mother's death.

She looked at Aidan and asked him to sit for a moment and that she had something she wanted Aidan to know.

What Ever Happened to Whitney Lake?

"I was barely ten years' old when my mother suddenly died. I am not sure how death is supposed to affect a young child, but I know what it did to me. My mother was in a loveless and abusive marriage, and I made a pact with myself not to repeat her life. I more-or-less raised myself from that time on, and I had no intention of depending on someone else to take care of me in the future."

Whitney was hoping that Aidan would understand her better, and the reason she was so reluctant to commit to a relationship. Her stomach was uneasy after saying what she did to Aidan. Maybe she just shouldn't have said anything at all, and let the past be just that.

Aidan just looked at her with an empty expression on his face. Most of his tan color had drained away and Whitney didn't know what he was thinking. It was a few minutes, and Whitney could see him still in deep thought. Then he finally responded, "I really don't need to know about your past. You are with me now, and I have no reason to be cruel or abusive to you. Leave the past behind. We'll move to Colorado where you are away from all the people who have influenced you; friends from your employment, and mostly the airline friends. They are no good for you."

Whitney was surprised by his insistence that she not see any previous friends. He really didn't understand why she told him about her mother. She just wanted him to understand that the commitment to him was not easy for her, and that she needed to remain self-sufficient. None of her friends had any influence on her, ever.

Was he thinking that she was having an affair or others were leading her astray, and maybe away from him? It was the age difference. Whitney was sure that was true. He liked the fact that she was so much younger than him, and yet he seemed to be jealous of her socializing with anyone that he referred to as, "beneath him". In many ways, Aidan was arrogant, but it was his way of trying to separate Whitney from anyone that he thought of as a threat. He would say that he was trying to raise Whitney up above all those in her past, and little by little, she removed herself from her old friends, especially from the airline. In any case, living in Colorado would certainly create a distance from everyone. He would often say, "You only need me from now on."

Aidan was right in one way about the airline friends. Whitney was occasionally seeing one of the flight crew when she first met Aidan. What Aidan didn't know was that this was someone who Whitney knew from her years of teaching dancing at Arthur Murrays. They would often go dancing together on their days off, or sometimes on a layover, if they were lucky enough to have a schedule together. Most male dancers are gay, and he was no exception. That was now three years ago and Aidan was still suspicious of her flying. She remembered when he started taking her to the airport for her few days' flight, and then picking her up when she returned. She suspected that he wanted to see the crew that was on her schedule.

At the same time, she put that behind her, and went ahead with the commitment, still being somewhat unsure of the unknown life in another state. Up until now, she and Aidan had feasted on adventure. Whitney began thinking of the move to Colorado as an exciting new way of life; a giant step into the unknown.

~

They settled on a ranch in the southwest Colorado Mountains. The valley was somewhat remote with ranches that raised cattle and that had enough water, either by irrigation or from the frequent afternoon showers. It was called the Wet Mountain Valley. Straight west of Pueblo, they drove over the foothills, and down into the lush green valley. The view was stunning, with an expanse of snowcapped mountains for miles, north and south; some of the peaks were up to 14,000 feet. The valley floor was almost flat with sizeable irrigated hay fields. Numerous small streams trickled out of the Sangre De Cristo Mountains that became the source of the

Angie Koenig Olson

flood irrigation. They learned about water and mineral rights being separate deeds in Colorado. A creek flowed through the ranch and down into the lower valley. Their ranch was second for water rights, so when the spring thaw bulged the creek, they had the right to open the flood irrigation gates. The mineral rights went with the land, but it wasn't a likely prospector's find.

The entrance to the ranch was at an elevation of 9,500 feet. Aidan liked the grandness of the ranch, with a total of 640 acres. About one-third of the land was flood-irrigated from the stream that flowed down the mountain and through the length of the property. He also liked the plateau next to the entrance. It was flat and long enough for a future runway for the Cessna.

Everything moved along quite quickly, and the next thing Whitney knew, she was a mountain girl, sleeping with the yelping of nearby coyotes, and waking to the sound of sheep baaing in the pasture outside their bedroom window.

Aidan said he would take care of selling her home back in the city, and he did, with her signing mailed papers and returning them back to the real estate broker in Minneapolis. She really wanted to keep her home, and have it as a place to stay when they returned to the city. But Aidan said they weren't going back and it was best to just have an apartment in the city when he needed to be there on business. He didn't want to be bothered with a single-family home to maintain. Whitney thought that was Aidan's excuse for not keeping her first home. Whitney knew he didn't like the house, mostly because it was something she had purchased on her own.

~

With a bit of a lump in her throat, Whitney had packed her personal possessions and boarded the Cessna for their new Colorado home. She was still a little uneasy about giving up her life in the city, but the decision had been made, and she and Aidan together would dive into this new adventurous life.

Chapter 14

They named the property, the High-Country Ranch, and installed a tall wooden sign above the cattle-guard-entrance. When anyone drove through the entrance, the view of the Sangre de Cristo Mountains was breathtaking. The realtor told them that a hiking/horse trail snaked through these mountains just inside the tree-line. The locals said that the Rainbow Trail traversed for over one-hundred miles, although the travel information said it was only 10 or 12 miles in length and was somewhat rough and rocky as it forked off to campsites and mountain lakes. They also boasted of the spectacular views all along the trail, the sweet aroma of the dense pine forest, and the deep azure-blue waters of the hidden mountain lakes.

~

They became instant ranchers, with part of the purchase agreement being that Aidan and Whitney allow the previous owner of the ranch to keep his flock of sheep grazing until late summer, or just after the sheep were to be sheared, and would then be sold at auction. The ewes seemed to feed on the grass in the lowlands next to the creek, and maybe the owner came by to check on the flock, but Whitney never saw anyone come by. Once in a while, she found herself having to rescue a young lamb that had slipped under the fence and the ewe would baa, baa, wanting the youngster back, but not know how to do so. The lambs were easy to pick up and slide back under the fence. The young needed the protection of the adults before nightfall, or they could become prey for the coyotes.

The nights were filled with the sounds of the coyotes howling and yipping, sometimes very close to the main house, and other nights, off in the distance. The young lambs were defenseless against these wild dogs. At times, after all the yelping, there was a prolonged silence. Whitney came to know what that meant.

What Ever Happened to Whitney Lake?

~

In the first part of August, an extra-long pickup truck arrived, pulling a 30-foot covered trailer. It was another beautiful windless day filled with bright sunshine. Six men jumped from the truck and began setting up fencing to guide the sheep into a line to the wool shearers. The shearing happened really quickly, as each animal was quite gently rolled from one side to the other, until each sheep was bare. The wool was tossed aside by the shearer and eventually gathered up and packed into gunny-sacks. The sheep didn't seem to fight the shearing, in fact, the shearers said that they liked it, and they remained quite calm through the rather quick ordeal. Competitors can shear an adult in under two minutes, but the shearing hands that Whitney watched at the ranch, took closer to three minutes—still amazingly fast to someone who had never watched the process before.

Under that extremely thick coat of wool, was this surprisingly skinny frame. The shearing had to be done early enough in the season, so there was still enough time for a new coat of wool to cover their bare skin before the cold weather set in.

What Ever Happened to Whitney Lake?

Within a few hours, a couple hundred sheep were huddled together for warmth, as the shearing was finished. The wool sacks were loaded into a covered trailer, and the shearers were gone, as quickly as they had arrived.

The next day, the naked sheep were loaded in trucks and they disappeared from the landscape. They were still good breeding stock, and the wool was still in high demand. The owner sent the herd off to auction, and Whitney supposed they would be purchased by another rancher, and would probably stay somewhere in the valley.

Whitney was still reminded of the sheep for many months after the animals left the ranch. The distinctive smell of sheep manure seemed to permeate all the surfaces, hard or soft. The linoleum floors in the ranch house's back hallway and closets smelled of sheep droppings, no matter how much scrubbing Whitney did. It was as if the smell had imbedded itself in the walls and the floors, and even the ceiling.

Chapter 15

The ranch house was nothing special or different; it was rather ordinary to Whitney. It was built using full logs and was one floor with four bedrooms and three bathrooms, a good-sized kitchen with a center island, and eating space next to the large picture windows that viewed the Sangre De Cristo Mountains for miles in both directions. The living room was a decent size with a wood-burning stone fireplace. It was a basic rambler, but Whitney would make it a home in no time.

Whitney drove to Pueblo and purchased paint brushes, drop-cloths and all the necessary supplies to start painting, room by room. The entire ranch-house really needed a fresh-clean look. Finding a painter in the valley was maybe possible, but she really needed something to do when she was alone that first summer.

Angie Koenig Olson

During the first few months at the ranch, Whitney and Aidan made several trips to Denver to find furniture for their house, including beds, linens and kitchen items. They had arrived at their new home with two suitcases and the clothes on their backs. What furniture Whitney had in her city home, Aidan moved to his apartment in town, including the white monster TV.

After being at the ranch for just a few months, Aidan was already needing more space. He wanted a separate area in the ranch house for a workout room, a sauna and family-room. They found local carpenters to transpose the existing garage into that family room, and to add on a work-out room and a new garage. The carpenters were not from the valley and drove the sixty miles each day to the ranch. It was a slow process, as all the lumber and materials had to come from Pueblo, or Colorado Springs, or even Denver. Within a few months, the addition was complete with a floor to ceiling twelve-foot-wide, obsidian glass, volcanic-rock fireplace. The obsidian was the only material that came from a local mine just a few miles from the ranch. Aidan seemed to think that bigger was always better. Whitney thought the fireplace was a bit over-the-top in size, as it dominated almost an entire wall of the new room.

~

Meanwhile, the outside view towards the mountains had been left natural with cactus and sage brush intermingling in the arid soil. Aidan hired a dirt mover who was also a local rancher. The rancher was a little concerned about disturbing the natural habitat. He calmly said to Aidan, "Up here in the mountains we don't disturb too much of the topsoil if not needed. It is the wind and the dry climate that we have to respect." Aidan didn't pay too much attention to what the rancher said, and he proceeded to have the land around the house reshaped and pushed back away where the terrain sloped towards the mountains. Another rancher agreed that he would supply trees that were grown in the area. The tree rancher stated that they had to come from within one-thousand feet of the same altitude, or they wouldn't survive.

Several trucks arrived with at least fifty beautiful spruce trees that were at least six feet tall. The next week the trees were planted across the newly terraced back yard along with a sprinkler system. No one thought of checking the water pressure before adding the new sprinklers, and they quickly found out that the current seepage well could not power the sprinkler heads. Everyone knew everyone in the valley and the dirt mover said he would check around for a well driller.

Shortly after the trees were planted, to Whitney and Aidan's surprise, the wind picked up like non they had experienced before. The morning air was still and wind free, but by noon, the wind gained strength as it came over the mountains and swooped down into the valley, often carrying a silt that hazed the air. The new trees were hanging on by guide-wires; this was the only way that they could survive the blast until they were well rooted into the rocky soil. That is when the newcomers to the valley discovered where all the sand in the air was coming from. The Great Sand Dunes National Park was just across the mountains in the San Luis Valley. The winds would whip across the dunes, picking up the fine sand and fly it across the mountain tops and down into the Wet Mountain Valley, and coat everything with a fine dust only a good rain would settle down.

When the new family room was completed, and floor-to-ceiling picture windows were installed to view the mountains and the new tree plantings, the winds were back and relentless. Not only did much of the topsoil disappear around the new tree plantings, but the new picture windows were sand-blasted by the high winds. It was somewhat like a Midwest snowstorm, when the winds whip around a building, piling snow in swirls around the house- corners.

Aidan and Whitney had no idea that the winds could do so much damage. Shortly thereafter, they had sod brought in to cover all the areas that they had skinned off and left to the mercy of the wind. They also realized they needed to have a better source for water than the seepage well that dribbled into a storage tank along the creek somewhere above the old original cabin. They knew the well was useless for trying to operate the sprinklers, so a new well had to be drilled quickly, or all the trees and sod would be a feast for the persistent wind.

~

It seemed as if everyone in the valley had more than one talent or profession. Most ranchers had other specialties. Ranchers or farmers can fix or do just about everything to make their land function without an outside service. Whitney was sure that the locals thought that they were 'the fools from the city'.

Aidan was told that the local bar was a good source for notes pinned up of services. They found a well driller who was available to drill, but said he need to have the water dowser come and find the best place to drill. Whitney had heard about this method of finding water, but thought it was only folklore and no one in these modern times needed to do anything like that to find a decent flow. Apparently, this was common practice for drilling in the mountains, but it was a new experience for both Aidan and Whitney. Aidan seemed leery about this whole process, but Whitney was excited to see how this was to happen.

Along the creek, there were an abundance of willows gracefully leaning across the water. The Witcher found a fairly long branch, about two feet or so with a forked shape so that he could hold each side and point the end forward. He held the willow branch, palms up, as he proceeded to walk around an area that would be good access for the well to the house.

What Ever Happened to Whitney Lake?

Whitney followed the Witcher around until he finally came across the right spot to drill the well. As he stood over the spot, his arms and hands were shaking as if he was having a violent seizure, until he could no longer hang on and dropped the branch to the earth. He was excited about the find and marked the spot for the drill rig to position its point. Apparently, the strength of the pull to the earth determines the quantity of water found. He suggested they install a four-inch casing that would fill all their future water needs. He couldn't tell them how deep he would have to drill, but he said the larger flows are usually deeper.

He asked Whitney if she would like to try dowsing, and she immediately said, "Yes, I would!" They walked back towards the creek where he knew she would find water. He cut a new branch for her and watched as she walked around the hay field and stopped as her hands began to shake, and then her arms, as she attempted to hold the branch upright, but she found it impossible as the point of the branch struggled to reach for the earth. In some ways, she was surprised, and then at the same time, she wasn't surprised at all.

The well rig man came the next day with a rather crude old piece of equipment. The man was short and greasy-looking, as if he hadn't showered in between drilling jobs. After a day of equipment set-up, he fired up the gasoline engine, and the drilling began. The driller stayed with his equipment day and night, and slept in a small tent that he set up next to the rig. In the evening, Whitney would open their bedroom window to hear the purring of the motor as the seemingly endless grinding continued twenty-four hours a day.

The driller stayed with his rig constantly, and Whitney wondered if he had enough to eat, so she started making an extra plate of food for the rangy man in the tent. He was always very grateful, with a big charitable smile and a tip of his soiled western hat.

He hit an aquifer at 100 feet, and said there most likely is a bigger flow down deeper, so he kept on drilling to about 125, and then hit a bigger source at about

What Ever Happened to Whitney Lake?

150 feet. It was some ten days later when the driller decided that was as good as it was going to get. It was a decent flow, but not as big as he anticipated. But, it was adequate, and the new well was hooked up to the ranch house and then to the much-needed sprinkler system to water the strained trees and grasses.

~

The TV reception was fair at best at the ranch, and the signal came from Pueblo, sixty miles away. Aidan wanted to increase the signal for better reception, so he hired another rancher who also had an RCA TV service in the valley. A jovial round-faced cowboy with spurs on his boots arrived at the door and greeted Whitney with, "Hello Ma'am, Your Mr. called about improving your TV reception." He tipped his hat to Whitney as he stepped inside the back door of the ranch-house.

Whitney quickly learned that cowboys tip their hat as a courtesy, but rarely take it off. In fact, they don't want anyone else to touch their Stetson. So, it stays on their head.

The RCA cowboy said it was best to install a tower that would pull in a better signal. He went on to say that the tower would help prevent signal interference from the foothills. Within a few days, the seventy-five-foot tower with a booster on the top stood high above the ranch house. A wire trailed from the top and into the garage and eventually to the TV. The reception was a little bit better, but still on the fuzzy side. The happy RCA cowboy said that another booster might help even more. Now the tower would have a booster to boost the booster. The RCA cowboy also added a device to point the antenna in different directions. The result was that the TV now picked up the same channels, but from Denver, Colorado and Albuquerque, New Mexico and other distant cities, with no better reception from any of them. Aidan finally gave up on improving the TV reception, and the few stations that were available came with a cloud of snow covering the screen, no matter which way the antenna was directed.

Chapter 16

About a half-mile west and closer to the mountains, but still on the ranch property, there stood the original log cabin that was in dis-repair, but had a charming setting next to the creek that meandered through the ranch. Aidan and Whitney decided to restore the old structure and modernize the interior. Eventually, they would be able to provide housing for the extra help needed to manage the ranch. After-all, Aidan knew nothing about raising cattle, or any farm animals. He was a city boy, and was used to hiring everything and everyone to get things done. Whitney never wanted to admit that she grew up on a farm in the Midwest that at one time had cows, pigs and chickens. As it was, she was very young when their farm had animals of any kind, and she certainly didn't know anything about raising beef cattle in the high country of Colorado.

~

Angie Koenig Olson

There really wasn't much to the old cabin structure, but they carefully had the building jacked up, only to find a number of skunks and other varmints that had made their home in the rock foundations and under the floorboards. They spread multiple bags of mothballs all around and under the cabin, hoping the critters would leave and find another home. A local handyman brought a cement mixer, set up concrete forms and began pouring the new footings. A week or so later, they set the log building back down on its new foundation, and started re-building the roof, then adding windows and doors and re-chinking the 100-year-old hand-scribed logs. Somehow, the carpenters were able to straighten the walls and square-up the window openings. They carved the interior into a two-bedroom abode with a kitchen/living room and one bathroom. In reality, it would have been far less expensive to have a fire and build a new structure where the old cabin stood. But it was good to save a piece of history and provide housing for a ranch hand.

An electrician who worked full-time for the county on the power lines, also did electrical work on the side for people like Aidan and Whitney. Most ranchers could supply their own electrical needs, but they were the city folks who had to rely on others for almost everything. A thin-framed weathered cowboy came to the house door with a string of rattlers dangling from his heavy leather belt. A hand gun was in a holster and Whitney was sure it was loaded. He said he always carried a gun for the rattle snakes in the dry hills where he mostly worked. He pointed to the rounded hills to the east, as he proudly shook the dozen or more rattlers that were hanging from his belt.

~

The lineman/electrician worked with precision, as he set new poles in the ground and attached the electric wire between the main house and the cabin. He wired the cabin and the new addition at the main house, and brought power to the new well. The water from the old seepage well would be adequate for all the water needs of the cabin. It was such a delightful setting. Whitney was just a little bit envious that the cabin had a much more inviting setting than the main house. When the windows were open, you could hear the creek constantly rustling across the rocks as it flowed mild-tempered down the mountain. When the irrigation flood gates were open, this was the water that flooded the ranches' hay-fields.

Before winter set in, the cabin was finished and ready to become home to a ranch manager, or maybe a cowhand.

At first, Whitney hadn't realized how far every service was from the High-Country Ranch. At that time, the whole county consisted of only about six hundred people, and it was one of the larger counties in Colorado.

What Ever Happened to Whitney Lake?

About ten miles away, there was a small town of a little more than a hundred citizens, including men, women and children. There was a small grocery store, a bar/restaurant and a service station, a school, a church and a medical doctor. After that, it was sixty miles to everything in various directions.

Aidan put the word out in town that they were looking for a ranch hand, and proceeded to tack a note up on a board at the local bar. It was just a few days later when a young man named Tim Palefeather stopped by the ranch. He came up to the back door, removed his hat and said he was looking for work, and said that he saw the note on the bulletin board. He was a very nice-looking boy, with sunned skin, thick coal-black hair, and soft brown eyes. His heritage was evident, being part Navajo and the other part Mexican. What he was didn't make any difference to Aidan or to Whitney. After all, the ranch was in southern Colorado, and they were the odd newcomers, with blonde hair and pale skin. The locals in town made a point of telling them of Tim's heritage as a bit of a heads-up. "Sometimes, he has a thirst that is uncontrolled." That was somewhat of an eye-opener, but Aidan was willing to give him a chance and hired him that same day.

He was a very polite young man, and removed his hat whenever he came to the door, and always called

Whitney Mrs.. He was the only cowboy so far who removed his hat at the door. Whitney thought, *He must really need the job.*

Tim and his new young wife moved into the log cabin by the creek, and were obviously delighted with this freshly re-built home.

For some reason, Whitney had thought Aidan knew something about ranching and raising cattle before they purchased the ranch. She quickly found out that he knew nothing and had to rely on hiring someone for everything. And Whitney considered herself a city girl, even if she had grown up on a farm.

How many cattle can the ranch support? That is how the realtors valued the land when it was put on the market. That number was about 100 head between the grazing land and the irrigated section along the creek for the winter feeding. So, Aidan would be sending Tim off to auction to purchase 100 whiteface yearlings for breeding, along with three bulls. First they had to build a stockade fence out of railroad ties to pasture the bulls. According to Tim, the plan would be to breed the 100 white-face heifers and sell their youngsters the next spring.

They had been at the ranch about a year when the cattle trucks arrived along with a separate truck with the bulls. Tim had all the yearlings released into the stockade-fenced pasture along with the three bulls, each weighing more than 2,000 pounds. What a show this was for Aidan and Whitney. Two of the huge bulls spent days and nights with locked horns while one bull was losing weight with all the breeding activity. Needless to say, less than half of the herd was bred the first year. It seemed that their ranch hand didn't know the only one bull per pasture rule. Once the bulls were in the pasture with the females, it became impossible to alter what was happening. Aidan and Whitney realized that Tim was maybe good at following directions when he was told what needed to be accomplished. It became evident that he also knew little about ranching. But, Aidan and Whitney needed someone to care for the livestock, and at that point, Tim was the only choice they had, so he stayed on.

Chapter 17

One late summer afternoon, Tim was on his way back to the ranch from the flat-lands near Pueblo. He was looking to purchase at least four cutting horses to manage the cattle in the various pastures. As he told the story, he was pulling a trailer loaded with two horses behind the ranch truck, when alongside the road, in the middle of nowhere, was a black and white dog that was curled up in the ditch. Tim didn't know if the animal was sick or hurt, so he picked him up and loaded him in his pickup, and brought him to the ranch. Tim proudly said, "I brought you a dog for the ranch. All ranches should have a dog." The dog was shivering, undernourished and seemingly afraid. Whitney smiled at Tim and at the scraggly pup, even if she wasn't sure where the dog actually came from. Tim said, "People will drop unwanted animals in the middle of nowhere. This one seems like a pretty nice dog."

They named him Nicki, and Tim built a dog house for him next to the barn. The dog appeared to be quite young, and was shy and afraid when he first came to the ranch, but eventually, Whitney could get close enough to pet his multi-colored head, or give him a treat. It seemed as if he had been abused by someone, and as Tim had said, just dumped off in the middle of nowhere. Within a few weeks, he became their dog and slept mostly on the front stoop of the ranch house.

Nicki was an Australian Shepherd breed, with one brown and one blue eye, and his calling was to round up the animals. First, it was the neighbor's sheep, as he ran back and forth behind the herd, barking his way around, until the sheep were all in one close-knit bunch.

Whitney would watch him from their front porch as he was eyeing the cattle as they spread out to graze in the early afternoon. She could almost read Nicki's mind—that he couldn't stay still any longer, he just had to be rounding up the herd into a tight circle. If they didn't move the way he wanted, he would nip their heels, encircling back and forth until maybe he was tired, and so were the animals. Sometimes he would be at this for an hour or so, and he had to be called in, or physically brought out of the pasture. It didn't matter if the animals were sheep or cows, the ritual was the same.

One late summer day, when Nicki had been at the ranch for a few months, he lost a battle with a porcupine. Whitney found him lying on the side of the driveway, moaning in agony with the sun beating down on his frail body, his mouth open, but unable to make a sound. The bloody porcupine quills were lodged inside behind his teeth, and propped his mouth open at least three inches. From the first day at the ranch, Nicki would never jump in a vehicle to go along with anyone; he would always shy away. Whitney was sure it was of the fear that he was going to be left in the middle of nowhere again. But this time, he was hurting so badly, that he let Whitney pick him up, and lay him in the back of the Bronco.

Whitney drove through the foothills and down the mountain to Pueblo (sixty-miles) where they asked a cowboy on the street if he knew of a veterinarian nearby, and he did. He said, "Follow me," as he hopped in his truck and motioned Whitney to follow. It was just a few short blocks to the vet, and the cowboy helped Whitney carry Nicki inside the office. His moaning had slowed, as if he was giving up. The vet knew how much pain Nicki was in, and gently laid him on the exam table, and gave him a shot of something to quiet him down, so he could start removing the quills from his mouth.

It was more than an hour before the vet was finished. The vet's forehead was dripping beads of sweat. Whitney knew it was almost as painful for the doctor as it was for the patient. Once the quills were removed, there was nothing much left to do to help him. Nicki's immune system would have to take over from here.

The cowboy had waited with Whitney until the vet was finished. He carried Nicki back to the Bronco and laid him down on a blanket. Whitney thanked him as he said, "I'm sure he will be just fine. That dog is a tough breed." He tipped his hat and left as quickly as he had appeared.

Nicki was quiet on the hour-plus trip back to the ranch, still groggy from the sedation. As soon as he sensed the entrance gate to the ranch, his head perked up a little, and his tail started slowly wagging. He knew that he was going back home.

What Ever Happened to Whitney Lake?

It took a week or so before he started to be his old self, when Whitney noticed he was once again eyeing the grazing cattle in the front pasture.

~

Whitney thought the ranch was a little sterile, for whatever was her reasoning. She asked Tim if there was a place in Pueblo that they could purchase a pair of geese and maybe have baby goslings? She wanted more life at the ranch and thought it would be good to see the geese parade around the yard with their babies trailing, and maybe swim in the pond that was next to the driveway. Whitney thought they might even like to venture up the creek.

Tim made the trip to Pueblo within a few days, and returned with a pair of white geese. As it turned out, the geese were not particularly friendly, and would hiss and chase everyone if they tried to approach them. Whitney had another thought, and decided to send Tim for some more friendly ducks. "Surely, they would be better than the geese."

Tim brought home a dozen white Peking ducks and set them sailing on the pond. Whitney thought that they were beautiful, swimming around, feeding on the bugs and grasses and the nightly corn that she would spill on the shore.

Then one morning, she noticed that there weren't twelve anymore, but only ten. A fox or a coyote must have taken them during the night. She really didn't have a pen to bring them inside, so she thought they would have to take their chances in the dark hours. Then, a few days later, Tim found two water-soaked duck-carcasses lying on the pond's shore. It seemed so strange that a wild animal would kill the ducks and leave them be.

Not more than a day later, Whitney was sitting outside looking at the pond when she noticed something very strange was happening. A goose was mounting the back of a duck and holding it underwater until the duck drowned. She couldn't believe what she was seeing. The two geese killed two more ducks that day. Later in the day, when Tim was back in the yard near the house, Whitney approached him and told him what she saw happening at the pond. Tim couldn't believe it either, but quickly headed down to the pond to pick up two more drowned ducks. Whitney asked Tim is he would like a goose dinner or two? Whitney said, "Go get your shotgun and get rid of the geese once and for all."

Whitney heard two shots ring out just before nightfall. In the morning, she noticed the geese were gone from the pond.

What Ever Happened to Whitney Lake?

The few ducks that were left, lasted through the summer, with fewer by fall and then none were seen again when winter came. Whitney's idea fell short of successful, and she decided not to try for the ducks again. She found it interesting that Nicki never tried chasing any of the ducks, or even the geese. She supposed he was a cattle and sheep dog only.

Chapter 18

In December of the first year living in Colorado, Aidan and Whitney's daughter was born. The hospital was in a small town some sixty miles from the ranch. Whitney was uneasy about the distance for medical help, but she took some comfort knowing that there was a lady doctor who practiced about ten miles away from their ranch, and she could assist in an emergency.

As it was, they made the sixty-mile drive to the hospital the night before, and the baby was born the next day in early afternoon. Whitney's baby was the only newborn in the nursery, so there were many gawkers staring through the window at this tiny child wrapped in a pink blanket. "Look, look, a new baby," the passersby would say. It was a very small hospital, with a dozen or so rooms and an attached medical clinic where Whitney's doctor practiced.

In just a few days Whitney and Aidan and the new baby were back home at the ranch with the massive responsibility of a new life to care for. It was the first time in many years that she thought about her mother, and wished she was here to help her with the transition from gallivanting around the world to settling down, as many referred to as necessary after having a child. Her mother had died when she was very young, and none of her sisters were close in any way. As it was, she had chosen a very different life thus far and she had found she had very little in common with any of her siblings. Whitney never babysat while she was growing-up, and she was the youngest of the eight children, so her siblings watched over her. They say it is all very natural but Whitney was the first to disagree. She supposed the people who made this statement were all theorists. She was not at all sure of herself with the newborn, and being so isolated at the ranch, the seclusion did not help her to feel at ease.

Whitney had purchased Doctor Spock's book on Baby and Child Care, and had read it cover to cover before the baby arrived. She never opened the book again because nothing seemed relevant.

The first night, Whitney stayed awake, listening for a cry or a whimper, so that she knew the baby was breathing. She had placed a bassinet in their bedroom so the baby was nearby through the night. After about a week, she was very surprised when the baby slept through the night. Whitney thought that something was surely wrong, but it wasn't. And so, motherhood started to fall into place as Whitney began feeling more assured that she was doing OK as a new mother.

~

Aidan was very anxious for them to have a child together, but it seemed more and more of his time was spent at his business, either traveling to Europe or other destinations around the United States. Most often, he was in the south, either in Tennessee, Louisiana or Florida. Whitney found herself alone at the ranch, with Aidan flying in and out without much concern for Whitney. Shortly after their child was born, Aidan left on business and was gone for almost a month. He had stayed until the baby was born, but was anxious to get back to his business. From then on, he was frequently away from the ranch for a week or two. At daybreak Monday morning, when the sky to the east was beginning to show light over the foot-hills, he'd head down to the airport, and he'd return after dark on Friday of the same week, or sometimes the next week. She was beginning to wonder if this was the life that she had signed up for.

~

But as it was, life continued on at the ranch with or without Aidan. Whitney was very capable of taking charge, but was getting lonesome for other friendships. The distance between ranches was at least ten miles, and it was not easy to develop friendships as a newly settled rancher. They were the city folks who had intruded on the typical high country Colorado rancher's life, and Whitney knew it.

Chapter 19

Tim Palefether seemed to stand taller as he took on the responsibility of the ranch. He liked the position of boss, and was given much leeway by Aidan to purchase whatever he needed for the spread. One of the horses he had purchased was a bucking horse from the rodeo, and Tim said that he was sure he could tame the bucker into being good for cattle.

It was a bright summer afternoon when Tim parked the truck and trailer in the middle of the yard, opened the back gate, and proudly unloaded the fine-looking grey quarter horse. He saddled the new horse with the ease of an experienced cowboy, while the grey stood still as if well trained. With one boot in a stirrup, Tim swung his other leg across the young horse and to his surprise, the bronco began bucking beneath Tim with the power of the rodeo, but with no cinch pulled tight behind his belly. The grey horse gave Whitney a show as he bucked around the ranch yard for a minute, then made his way to the pond next to the driveway. Then the bucker lowered his head and Tim took flight across the rocky pond-shore and into a few feet of water.

Angie Koenig Olson

Tim managed to keep his composure somewhat, while he picked up his Stetson and trudged to shore and proceeded to empty the liquid from his boots while spitting out a little of the foul water from his mouth. He brushed away the grasses that were hanging on his blue jeans as he tromped across the yard where the calm bucker was standing. Whitney knew little about rodeo horses, except that a horse usually bucks because of the cinch they pull tight close to its back legs. In this case, the horse just bucked because someone was on its back.

Tim didn't say a word but quietly loaded the horse back into the open trailer. The next morning, he left the ranch at first light, and headed back down the mountain road to give the grey-bucker a different home.

Whitney had heard about the rodeo that was just outside of town the next weekend, and she wondered if

What Ever Happened to Whitney Lake?

Tim had purchased the bucker so that he could show off his bronco riding skills.

Whitney didn't know why they had to have at least four quarter horses all the time. Tim said that horses tire and you should always have fresh horses. That seemed like a feeble excuse to Whitney, for there was very little reason to round up cattle when the pasture land was fenced.

~

The only bar in town was frequented by many of the ranch workers on Friday and sometimes Saturday evenings. Some stayed too long at the bar, and tempers very easily flared with the fuel of too much whiskey. Somehow, most cowhands became stronger, braver or just plain out of control by midnight.

One Saturday morning, the phone rang—the young ranch manager was in jail for punching the local sheriff. Apparently, Tim had been in an active fist fight with another local when the sheriff attempted to split up the cowboys. The lawman got in the middle of the two fighters, and Tim socked him, sending the lawman over backwards and sprawled out on the boardwalk outside the bar. Maybe he didn't mean to punch the sheriff, but it happened in the heat of the fight, and Tim had to make restitution for his actions.

Angie Koenig Olson

The next morning, the sheriff calmly explained what had happened the night before, and told Aidan that he had the boy behind bars. It was going to cost a few hundred dollars to release him. Aidan grumbled a little but ended up paying the fine, and gave Tim another chance. With his head down, Tim appeared at the ranch-house backdoor, and was very apologetic for what had happened, saying over and over again; "I am so sorry, so sorry, it won't ever happen again."

But it did. About a month later the same type of bar-fight ended up with another sock at the sheriff, this time busting out a few of the lawman's teeth, and the Sheriff was hopping mad.

It was sad, but when Tim was arrested a second time, the ranch had to let him go. Aidan did pay his bail to get out of jail, but told Tim that it was best that he left the valley. He and his wife packed up their possessions from the log house, and that same day they disappeared as quickly as they had arrived. The raised eyebrows and the heads-up concern of the locals should have alerted Aidan, and maybe they did, but he thought he would give him a chance and possibly he had changed his habits.. Everyone in the valley apparently knew about Tim's problems with the bar and alcohol.

What Ever Happened to Whitney Lake?

Aidan didn't waste any time hiring a replacement as manager, and the new man would be arriving in about a week.

~

Meanwhile, the cattle had the creek for water and plenty of grass and hay for feed. The horses had hay and water in the corral, but Aidan said that they should find some oats in the barn. "Horses love oats," he said. Aidan and Whitney looked around and found a covered barrel, and having looked inside, found it was half full of oats. Aidan scooped out a quarter of a pail and held it up to the first horse, then repeated until all the horses had the oats as a treat. Little by little, all four started to shiver and shake and started heaving and gasping for air. Two of the horses fell down, and kept trying desperately again and again to get up on their wobbly legs. They finally succumbed, and lay helplessly gasping for air with expanded bellies. The two that were less aggressive were still standing, but shaking violently as they struggled to remain upright. Whitney ran to the house and called the veterinarian, but he had to drive up from Pueblo. It was at least two hours before they saw his Bronco speeding up their long driveway.

Aidan and Whitney had no idea what had happened, except something must have been wrong with the oats. The vet looked at the failing animals and said they had apparently eaten some poison. He began flushing the systems of the two that were still standing. The two that were already lying down were beyond help. The most aggressive one that had to be in front and ate the most poisoned grain, was the first to expire.

The vet was able to save two of the quarter horses, but from that day on, both horses' temperament was different. They spooked easily and were hard to get close to. The vet said they probably had some brain damage and would never be the same as before they ate the poisoned oats.

Apparently, the ranch had had a barrel of poison for the mice and maybe even rats, but the previous owner never told Aiden about it. It seemed so careless that the poison-oat barrel was left unmarked.

The next day, two cowboys came with a bobcat and dug a single grave on the upper part of the land for the two 1,000-pound horses that didn't survive. They picked up rocks from the creek and formed two crosses to mark the graves. The cowboys stood silent for a moment with their hats across their hearts. When they finished the burial, the cowboys left the ranch with the poison barrel in the back of their pickup

What Ever Happened to Whitney Lake?

It was so sad and unnerving for Aidan and Whitney. They couldn't get it out of their heads that they were responsible for killing two of their own horses, and left the other two with physical and temperament problems. Most of the time the two that survived the poison just stayed in the corral, looking listless and had to be coaxed to eat even their hay.

~

It was shortly after the horse poisoning, when the veterinarian was called again.

The whiteface cattle were all in one of the dry pastures grazing next to the creek, until Whitney noticed a few of the herd had somehow jumped the fence and were in the alfalfa and clover field. This field was not normally grazed until the last cutting was off the field, just before snow. That was the irrigated field that was cut for the winter hay. It wasn't long before Whitney noticed that two of the whiteface had collapsed and looked as if they couldn't move.

Being she had just been through the horse-poisoning, she was wondering if they had been poisoned also. She quickly called the veterinarian who happened to still be in the valley and he came to the ranch within the hour.

The vet knew exactly what was wrong, and quickly put a breathing tube down the almost lifeless cow, and proceeded to make an incision through its hide above the stomach area. He then inserted a tube that would let the gas buildup out of the animals' rumen. The Vet said, "Cattle can't have very much green clover or alfalfa. They have an unusual digestive system, and gas can build up in this part of their stomach, and it will eventually cut-off their air supply. It is best to not let them graze in the fresh field."

The vet was able to rescue one of the cows, but the other one was beyond saving. Aidan and Whitney's inexperience on a ranch had killed another beautiful animal from what is known as cow's bloat. The vet said he would have someone help with burying the dead animal somewhere on the ranch property. The same two cowboys that had buried the horses, came with their bobcat and picked up another 1,000-pound carcass and headed up to the upper end of the land to where the horses were buried. As they were driving to the upper part of the ranch to dig another hole, one of the cowboys commented, "It is beginning to look like a cemetery up here."

Chapter 20

The ranch life was much different than what Whitney had expected. Somehow, she had thought that she and Aidan were going to live together in the mountains; At least, that is what she thought he said. But, in reality, she was fooling herself thinking that would happen. After all, he had business all around the US and Europe. Was she that naïve to think that he was going to change? Instead, she found herself without companionship more often than not. She gave up who she was, and most importantly, who she had become on her own. She had never imagined that Aidan would continue with his wandering lifestyle. Had she sold her soul? She would have to make the best of it for now. After all, she had a baby daughter and the ranch was not without surprises, with all the trials and tragedies.

Chapter 21

By now, they had been living at the ranch for more than a year, and Whitney found that Aidan was away almost weekly. He'd fly into Pueblo and drive sixty-miles up to the ranch late on Friday, and most times, leave again on Sunday afternoon.

The new ranch-manager arrived and Whitney was pleased that there would be other life at the ranch.

The new man came with a wife and a teenage daughter, and they moved into the cabin on the creek. Jack Meek was a retired military man who took direction with razor-sharp action. Meek was barrel-chested and had a round friendly face that smiled whenever he talked, but had the proper training not to stare into a superiors' eyes. Whitney thought he would be easy to be around and a welcome addition to the ranch. His wife was small and quiet, and seemed happy with their newfound log home, but Whitney knew that she would not be much companionship for her.

~

Aidan wanted to be in the thoroughbred horse business and Meek had apparently looked after the horses in the military, and had a depth of knowledge in birthing, raising and training horses. With Meek's recent retirement from the army, he was looking for other employment, and the High-Country Ranch was perfect for their family. Aidan told Meek that he had this idea that if you raise and train a horse at this high altitude, the horse will develop a larger lung capacity and will have an advantage over horses raised at sea level. Meek's eyebrows raised a little, he hesitated, and then said, "It's sure worth a try." Whitney didn't think that Meek thought too much of the theory, but he wasn't in charge, and he certainly was interested in trying out Aidan's idea. "Maybe it could make a difference," Meek said.

So, they built a barn with a dozen stalls for these exquisite thoroughbreds and began purchasing yearlings to train at this high altitude.

What Ever Happened to Whitney Lake?

Churchill Downs, Kentucky was considered the best thoroughbred horse auction in the country. It is also home to the Kentucky Derby—the most prestigious race in the United States. It was the first time that Whitney had been there, and as of yet, had not been to a horse race. It was also one of her first times to be away from the ranch in more than a year. It was wonderfully new and exciting. Mr. Meek, Aidan and Whitney sat in the bleachers around a small arena, as one by one a horse-for-sale was paraded by the bidders. Purchasers had time before the auction to look the horses over, and as Jack Meek was the authority, he told Aidan which horses to bid on and at what price. The auctioneer knew who the bidders were, and there were no hands raised or paddles with a number. The purchase was made with just a slight nod of the bidder's head. Aidan said to Whitney, "Don't move while the bidding is going on, or you may buy a horse."

They left the sale having purchased a half-dozen horses, some that had never raced, and some that had a short history on the track.

Before the horses arrived, the ranch was busy with an earth-grader grooming a stretch of high-ground into a quarter mile training track. Loads of a sand mix was smoothed out around the track and would be raked daily.

At daybreak, the young horses would be exercised and track trained for head and neck leads, and most of all, just learn to behave and follow the trainer's commands.

Whitney watched Meek, who with the skill of an artist, patiently began getting a yearling horse accustomed to having weight on its back. He began the process to eventually saddle the young horse ever so slowly. First a light blanket was placed across his back, then a heavier one, then two blankets, and often Janie, Meek's daughter, would lay across the horse's back, and finally the jockey's saddle. Janie as a teenager was as good with the horses as Meek. Each addition of weight was followed with a generous parade around the barn. More weight was added each day until a rider was finally mounted. All through the process, the young horse's ears were peeled back, a sign of apprehension about what was going on. This process took a number of days, and it could be weeks if the horse was skittish.

There wasn't any bronco-breaking as they seem to do with the western horses. By the time the rider was on the horse's back for the first time, the horse hardly noticed the difference, and walked along with a lead with little if any complications.

Meek built a starting gate out of steel so as to get the youngsters accustomed to the gates at the track. In the late afternoon, as the sun was slipping behind the mountains, one by one the horses were brought out of their stalls to be brushed down and fed grain before nightfall. Hay was always available in each stall for the horses to eat at their leisure. In the early morning, Whitney enjoyed hearing a horse or two whinnying from the barn above the house while they were being saddled for their morning workout.

Whitney rarely was able to go to any of the tracks where their horses were entered into a race, except the Centennial Race Track in Littleton, Colorado. She quickly learned that the racing game is an endless circuit. Once a horse is trained, it lives on the road, and moves from track to track and wherever the horse meets the qualifications for their races. The different tracks around the US each have their open times, mostly based on their normal weather patterns.

As it was, the ranch had a horse now and then that was in the money, but the high-altitude didn't seem to improve their performance. It was like anything else. Many would say, "The horse has heart. That kind of horse is a winner and is almost always in the money. It's the heart that counts most." Whitney thought that that was true. Some horses just loved being on the track and sensed that it was time to race and to be in the front of the pack. Once in the starting gate, a great horse became a different animal and was bound for the winner's circle. Others seemed to be satisfied with running at a good pace and just being in the pack. Some, just didn't have the heart or stamina to be a winner.

~

When Jack Meek came to the ranch, he brought along a mare that he owned, and he was hoping to breed this mare to a registered stallion with good lineage. He was also expecting to someday see this offspring race at some of the major tracks around the country. The mare was bred in February, and they all waited the eleven months with high hopes of a beautiful offspring.

The next year in late January, the ranch was buzzing with expectations of the upcoming birth. Whitney was no exception. She'd peek in the stall several times a day where the mare was kept to see if it was time. From the first part of the month, the lights were on nightly in the barn while the family switched over to a watch schedule.

Whitney rushed to the barn in early evening when the word came that it was time. It was a few hours before the new foal actually appeared. Because the thoroughbred delivers such a large foal, she is supervised day and night until she delivers. And so it happened, and the mare gave birth in the ranch barn on a soft bed of freshly cut hay, in the middle of the night. Meek and the other ranch-hand helped pull the baby out of the mare to reduce the stress and shorten what could be, a lengthy birthing. Whitney learned that all thoroughbreds are born as close to the first of the year as possible, so that they can hopefully qualify for a two-year-old race the next year, with x-rays to show that their leg joints were mature enough to race. If born later in the year, they may have to wait for a three-year-old race.

The skinny young foal immediately worked on standing up, falling numerous times until he was finally upright on his long spindly legs.

Meek looked at the beautiful new colt and looked over at Janie and said, "It is your horse Janie." She couldn't have been more delighted, with a smile as wide as her face.

It wasn't long before the young horse and mare were out in the pasture together, playing in the spring sunshine. The colt was born in late January, so he was now a couple of months old. He would nurse from the mare, and then would be off on his own, running and kicking and finding his new strength and agility, with the Sangre De Cristo Mountains as a backdrop. Whitney could see this pasture from the main house, and the antics of the youngster brought a new sense of excitement and contentment to her. The colt seemed to have that effect on everyone at the ranch. Even neighbors would stop by, wanting to get a glimpse of this beautiful thoroughbred.

What happened next, was totally surreal to Whitney. First she was watching the colt playing and tossing something in the air over and over, and then he laid down and started chewing. The next thing she saw was the young horse lying on its side, wildly kicking its hooves, obviously in distress, and gasping for air. Meek must have been watching the colt's antics too, and when the youngster laid down, Meek stopped what he was doing, and went running across the pasture, just in time to witness the colt catching his last breath.

What Ever Happened to Whitney Lake?

The colt had apparently picked up a piece of hard rubber in the pasture, and was chewing on it almost like a dog chews on a bone. It wasn't long before the colt got the rubber stuck in its throat, and was fiercely thrashing, unable to expel the rubber as it blocked the colt's airway.

There was obviously nothing Meek could do, but try to push on his throat over and over, trying to free the colt's obstructed airway. It was too late, and Whitney watched a tormented Meek lie down next to the colt while wiping away uncontrollable tears. Whitney thought it was best to just let him be. He stayed there until the sun was sinking behind the mountain peaks. He could see the dust following the yellow school bus about a mile away, as it came to a stop at the ranch entrance. The doors opened and Janie jumped off, anxious to be back at the ranch and to see the young colt. When Janie saw Meek lying in the pasture with the colt, Meek stood up and told her to go back home to their cabin, there was nothing they could do.

At daybreak the next morning, Whitney walked with Meek as he headed to the upper land on the ranch. Meek had wrapped the colt in a canvas and gently laid the carcass over the back of one of the ranch horses. He grabbed the reins and walked slowly, leading the horse up the land to where others were buried. He said he wanted to hand dig the burial hole himself. As a military man, Meek did the job in a robotic way, but with tears of grief that Whitney would never forget. Whitney decided to let Meek be alone for a while, and headed to the creek to gather rocks for another cross.

The plots in the upper part of the land did indeed become the ranch cemetery, with stone markers for each fallen animal.

~

There was a somberness that blanketed the ranch for weeks after this regretful event.

All the anticipation for the colt that Meek and Janie had had, was gone. That magic was now blown away in the wind; it was a bad and unexpected storm that came down on the land from nowhere. All the fun and excitement of raising and training horses had suddenly been put on hold. It would take a while for the shock of this death to be relegated to the past.

~

However, the ranch had other horses to care for, which was probably better for Janie. Whitney told Janie that she could have her personal horse, it she wanted it. The horse in question was more suited for a young girl anyway. It was a horse for which the time trials were too slow for the track, so it was brought back to the ranch to be just a potential riding horse. It would take a few years before that young horse would be calm enough to trust on a trail-ride. Whitney said, "The horse only knows one thing, when a bell rings, she runs. Janie, you will have to break her of that drilled-in habit."

Janie said, "I will, I will have her calmed enough to ride in no time."

Early the next morning, Whitney noticed Janie was already at the barn, parading her horse around for the morning exercise. Whitney was delighted to see how Janie's spirit had changed with the thought of her having a horse of her own.

~

The ranch always had an abundance of horses. Some would undergo time trials, usually at the Centennial Track in Littleton, and if their time wasn't fast enough to be entered in a race, they'd be brought back to the ranch for further training. Others, would come back because of an injury and needed to rest and to heal.

The ranch had one lead pony that actually was an older Tennessee walker named Cocoa. He was a big, smart and gentle horse that Whitney loved to ride. Because of his mild nature, they would send him to the race-track to lead young horses to the starting gate. After a few months of tugging on these adolescents, Cocoa would have to be brought back to the ranch to recuperate. It would take him a few weeks to settle down and regain his docile personality.

Whitney never cared too much about riding the horses that came back from the racetrack. They were high-strung and jittery most of the time. She would say, "Don't ring a bell or I will be off galloping for at least a mile." At the same time, she admired the thoroughbreds and the whole process of training and getting them ready to eventually race.

Chapter 22

At one time, when Meek was running the ranch, they had an extra ranch hand who lived in a trailer close to the main house. There was also a high-school age boy named Ray, who would sometimes come for the day if there was work for him.

The cowboy who lived in the trailer house would sometimes not be seen for a few days, and on a particular Monday morning, Mr. Meek told Ray to go to the trailer and roust MG out of bed. This cowhand seemed to drink too much whiskey, and apparently Meek had told him he would be finished if he was drunk again, and to be gone by Monday morning. His rusty and dusty Ford pickup was still parked next to the trailer, the same place it had been all weekend.

When Ray knocked on the door there was no answer. He knocked again and still no answer. So, he felt the door handle, and it was unlocked. He decided to open the door and peek inside to see if MG was still asleep. As soon as the door began to open, Ray could see MG's skeleton-like body, sitting in a chair with his cowboy hat tipped back. He was facing the door, with a pistol solidly pointed at his head. MG didn't waste any time doing what he had planned. A shot rang out as the door swung open, and blood quickly spurted from MG's temple in rhythm with the beat of his heart. Ray couldn't believe what he was seeing and backed out of the trailer stumbling and screaming as he turned and ran to the main house.

Whitney heard the shot from inside the house and was heading to the back door when she met Ray running up the walk. He was crying out, "He shot himself, MG shot himself, just as I opened the door."

Whitney told Ray to go and get a stack of clean towels from the bathroom, and use the house phone to call the sheriff and tell him that they needed the doctor and an ambulance.

She grabbed the towels and ran to the trailer where MG was slumped over in the chair, and apparently unconscious, with blood pulsing from his head. She wetted down the towels and began applying pressure to the wound while MG moaned like Nicki did with the porcupine quills stuck in his mouth. The smell of alcohol was strong on his breath and Whitney wasn't sure why he was semi-conscious. Was it the whiskey or the bullet?

It was more than thirty minutes before the doctor and the hearse/ambulance arrived. The doctor was the lady doctor from town and entered the trailer and saw

What Ever Happened to Whitney Lake?

Whitney sitting on the floor in the trailer-house with MG's head across her lap. Both were covered red with MG's blood. The doctor took one look at MG and said, "Oh, him again." She said that she had treated him before for this same similar attempt at suicide that she claimed was just to get some attention and sympathy. Whitney explained to the doctor that Meek had informed MG that he had to leave, and that his job was finished. Whitney explained to the sheriff that another ranch-hand went to see why he hadn't left, and just as he called out to him and opened the door to this trailer, he shot himself in his temple with a hand-gun. The boy who found him was obviously shocked and upset by what he just witnessed and came running to get help. Whitney said that she attempted to control the bleeding with compresses of wet towels while waiting for medical help. When the doctor arrived she said to Whitney, "Good job, on stopping the bleeding. He is more saturated with alcohol than he is unconscious from the gunshot-wound." They loaded him in the back of the multi-use/station wagon. Dead or alive, that was the town vehicle.

After the doctor left, Whitney looked around the trailer to find it littered with piles of empty whiskey bottles and loaded guns leaning against the walls and on the eating table. Something would have to change here; she couldn't have someone living so close to the main house with an ammunition stash and the endless bottles of liquor.

~

That was a rough time for Whitney, normally a pillar of strength. Her first thought was that of the safety of her child who was less than a year old.

Once again, Aidan was gone when this all took place, but he returned a few days later. He didn't press any charges but signed a restraining order against MG, saying he was not allowed anywhere near the ranch or in Custer County from then on. This apparently was his third try for attention with one of his weapons. The doctor said, "He knows just how to position the gun so that it will graze his temple and not be deadly. Meanwhile, those who find him feel responsible for his wounds, and pamper him, even if it is for just a short time; to him it was a success."

Whitney was shocked and shaken by the events of that day. Shocked by the desperate ranch hand who would stoop to shooting himself for attention, and shaken by the arsenal of weapons and mounds of whiskey bottles that occupied the trailer, less than 100 feet from her ranch-house door.

~

What Ever Happened to Whitney Lake?

The next day, Whitney woke up scratching her stomach, and her back was itching fiercely. She drove the Bronco the ten miles into town to see the doctor who had treated the gun-shot guy. The doctor looked at Whitney's stomach and then at her back, and smiled, and almost laughed and said, "It is probably a nervous reaction to what happened yesterday with the shooting." Whitney had a good case of the hives. The doctor said, "It will take about a week for the itching and redness to go away." She handed Whitney a prescription for the itching, if she needed it, or suggested over-the-counter itch cream that would do just fine.

When Aidan finally came up the mountain on Friday, he took one look at Whitney and said, "You look awful. How long will it take for all the bumps and redness to go away?"

She couldn't answer. He seemed so unconcerned about the danger. She doubted if he would be the great protector if he had been at the ranch. His nature was to have someone else take care of it, and in this case, was Whitney

Chapter 23

Every few weeks, Whitney begam to travel back to the city with Aidan on a Monday and return to the ranch on Friday or Saturday. The lack of companionship at the ranch was wearing on her, and she needed to either have company at the ranch, or spend more time in the city. She was tossed between these two worlds. She actually liked many aspects of the ranch, especially after she had been in the city for a few days. The quiet and peacefulness was a welcome relief from the busy city. She began to understand why Aidan liked the ranch. It was his escape from the pressure and congestion of the city and from his business. On occasion, she would travel with Aidan to his business destinations, but found herself more often than not, sitting in a motel room for most of the day, waiting for Aidan to finish his business. Whitney still stayed at the ranch most weeks, and just occasionally went to their city apartment. The apartment was cold and lifeless with little reason to want to be there, unless she was going to visit with some of her old friends. Further, Aidan was still insisting that she not see any of the people in her past life. He would make a point of saying that she was above them now, and didn't need anyone but him. But that wasn't true for Whitney. She would sneak off to lunch with a friend and not tell Aidan, but somehow he seemed to know that something was different about her. Maybe she appeared too happy or she was just acting differently. She wasn't really very good at role playing.

Whitney started asking friends and relatives to come visit at the ranch. She would say; "Please, please stay a week or so." And friends did come and some stayed the better part of a week.

Most of the guests who came enjoyed riding, so they would saddle up the cutting horses and head up into the mountains and onto the Rainbow Trail. Without exception, everyone thought the view was the best anywhere, and the peace and quiet was to be envied. Whitney would tell the guests that is was best to head out riding in the early morning. The clouds would often thicken by noon, and the winds would swirl around like an animal seeking out its prey. A storm could develop by early afternoon, out of nowhere it seemed.

Meek would have all the horses saddled and ready to go just after dawn. They'd pack a sandwich lunch and stop about midday next to a high-meadow and let the horses rest and graze. They ate their simple lunch while inhaling the sweet-smell of the Colorado pines that were softly whispering above.

What Ever Happened to Whitney Lake?

Hippies were sometimes camped along the trail with makeshift tents of canvas strung on ropes between trees. Sparsely clothed dirty children ran freely around the meagre campfire while the adults just lay around seemingly doing nothing. The air was pungent with smoke from either the fire or from them smoking weed. The hippies paid little notice of the riders who came close to their camp.

Whitney thought how simple and free their lives were, up here in the mountains, living off of the animals they would hunt and whatever berries were ripe along the path. Occasionally, Whitney would see one of the men in town, sprawled out on the boardwalk outside the only bar in town. Usually the still body was asleep, or pretending to be asleep, but with a sign saying, "Money for Food." Sometimes, a long-haired and bearded man would be playing the guitar with an open case for donations. Whitney would drop a few dollars in his case and receive a smile and a nod of appreciation.

When the guests packed their bags and headed down the mile driveway with the dust clouding behind their auto, again the ranch would feel sadly empty. Whitney was having anxious feelings about how long she could live this way, up here in this beautiful but isolated mountain valley.

Chapter 24

Aidan was often off to Europe, and would make sure he brought Whitney an extraordinary gift from his jaunts. There were two beaded evening clutch-purses from Belgium, an alligator clutch with a ruby clasp from France, and a diamond ring from somewhere that was to become her wedding ring. One time, Whitney didn't hear from Aidan for about three weeks. She was beginning to think that something must have happened to him. Surely, a phone call, even from Europe was obligatory if he planned to stay away that long? Somehow, Whitney didn't think that he thought that was necessary, or that he gave it any thought that he should contact her.

When he disappeared for the three weeks, he was supposedly in Italy, and a business associate asked if he was interested in going to Israel. Of course, he said yes. While being in the Middle East, he was told that his friend could arrange for them to travel to the Suez Canal, where constant military action was in process. As Aidan told the story, the Israeli army dressed him up in a military uniform with the intent of crossing the desert in a camouflage army jeep that would eventually travel to the Suez Canal. There could be a number of check-points along the way, and he was told to not say a word if they were stopped for inspection. They were stopped, and he kept his eyes low and away from the armed military.

Somehow, he survived that somewhat dangerous adventure and was excited to tell Whitney about it when he returned to the ranch. He finally called from New York with this big and exciting news. She was beginning to think that she was supposed to be living vicariously through his adventures, while before she was part of the exciting destinations. Their travels together had all but disappeared. That jaunt to Israel produced a gift of a cocktail ring with eighty small diamonds surrounding a single blue sapphire. Whitney did, indeed, think it was beautiful.

She was wondering if she would ever wear the massive cocktail ring. At least, not if they continued to live at the ranch. Aidan seemed to think that a gift was enough to keep Whitney happy, or at least keep her from asking too many questions about his globetrotting.

~

It seemed as if the ranch idea and living in Colorado was fading more in Whitney's eyes, and she thought in Aidan's as well. He was away more and more and Whitney sensed that he may be having some business problems, but he kept that part of his life to himself.

By now, the thoroughbred horses were mostly at racetracks around the country, and outside of a horse needing a rest at the ranch, the barn was empty. Aidan didn't have plans to purchase additional young horses to train, so the need for Meek's skills were dwindling.

As quickly as the ranch life unfolded before Whitney's eyes, it was fading into just a place to live in the Wet Mountain Valley. The runway to land the Cessna was never built, so Aidan had continued to commute to the Pueblo Airport and drive the sixty miles up to the ranch.

Then on a Friday in the spring, some four years later, Aidan came to the ranch from Pueblo and said, "I need to sell the ranch." Whitney wasn't really surprised, after all, the time he spent enjoying the ranch was minimal, and he needed to pay more attention to his businesses.

Whitney was elated, thinking of moving back to the city. Aidan said he had contacted the realtor who had sold him the ranch, and the realtor said that he thought he had a buyer for the property. Aidan probably thought that Whitney just lived there, and would have nothing to do with the sale. That was really true, because she was told that the ranch was titled to Aidan's company corporation.

And so, it was. The buyer was a local rancher and he was purchasing the property for his son who he thought needed a ranch to straighten his life out. Aidan and Whitney didn't ask what that meant, but they could guess. The buyers came to look at the property and said, "We'll take it."

Meanwhile, they had told Meek that the ranch was being sold, and that they needed to sell the cattle and cutting horses within thirty days. Meek said he would take care of everything. He also put the word out to the horse-people that he was available, and already had a number of job offers in Kentucky. It all fell into place like it was meant to be.

Trucks moving the cattle and the quarter horses drove in and out of the ranch for the next two weeks. It seemed all too quickly that the ranch was void of animals. Suddenly, the land felt very empty. Whitney hadn't realized what life the animals brought to the land, and now it just consisted of buildings with no purpose.

The ranch buyer said he would like the Australian Shepherd, if Whitney wanted to leave him. It was hard to leave Nicki, but this was his home, and they didn't have a place for him in the city. Whitney would never forget Nicki, and was hoping the new owner would bring some cattle on the property quickly, so that Nicki would have something to herd or just to chase. Although it was difficult to leave him, it was his home, and Whitney felt that the boy that was going to live there would be good to him.

Whitney packed up this Chapter in her life and left Colorado a little torn. She was wondering if anyone she knew had heard the coyotes howling, or watched sheep being sheared, or cattle breeding, or a goose drowning a duck, or the pain of porcupine quills in a dog's mouth, or poisoning of your own horses, or a young horse choking to death right in view in your pasture, or a cowboy shooting himself for attention? Those were just some of the vivid memories she would take with her forever.

~

They left all the furnishings in the ranch house, and boxed up only their personal effects and had the packages sent out via UPS.

~

One mid-summer day, In early morning, they drove down the mountain road the sixty miles, signed papers at the realtor's office and headed to the airport.

It was a perfectly clear day when they boarded the Cessna in Pueblo. After takeoff, Aidan climbed to an altitude high enough to look over the foot-hills to the west. Then he banked the plane for one last look at the Wet Mountain Valley and the Sangre De Cristo Mountains. Whitney thought she saw Aidan's eyes tear a little, as she wiped her own eyes, wondering if she would ever return to this valley.

Part III

Three Years Later

Chapter 25

Whitney found herself sitting in an attorney's office, in fact it was Aidan's company attorney. She leaned back in the over-stuffed leather chair and waited for the silence to break. Behind a gleaming mahogany desk was a Jewish man with slick-backed black-hair and a well-fed body. Whitney had met him once before when she and Aidan were married at the court house. His face was kind and he seemed concerned as he leaned across his broad desk and looked at Whitney. He hesitated, then asked, "Do you think there is any hope for your marriage, maybe counseling?"

She answered after a long hesitation. "No, I don't think so. After we moved back to the city, I thought our marriage would improve, but it didn't. It is best that we live separately so I can start having a real life again."

"What do you think went wrong?"

Whitney hesitated, then slowly said, "Everything changed after we moved to Colorado. Now, looking back, our relationship was starting to become strained even before that time."

"At first, it was all so magical, we were traveling and feeling as if we left the earth together. I was floating on a cloud. Then he kept after me to quit flying and he wanted me to settle-down, as he referred to it. But what he really meant was for me to settle down and be a housewife while he still had his freedom. He thought that keeping me isolated would somehow keep me faithful to him. I misjudged his words. I couldn't understand why he mistrusted me. When we first met, sure I had male friends. I suppose he expected me to immediately drop all my friends for him. After a few months of knowing Aidan, he was the only man in my life."

There was a silence for a few moments, as both Whitney and the attorney gathered their thoughts.

Whitney continued. "I rarely knew where he was, and he seldom called to see how we were. After our daughter was born, he was less and less at the ranch in Colorado. Our life as it was previously, had disappeared outside of skiing a few times at nearby ski areas. When we finally sold the ranch, I thought our life would get better together, but it didn't. Now that we were back in the city, the lack of trust had grown to the point of Aidan wanting to know where I was at all times and with whom. It seems he has never trusted me, ever."

Whitney was silent for a few moments, and then she continued, "I left Whitney behind when I married Aidan, and I have to get her back, even if that takes leaving him. Everything I have done and everyone I have wanted to see, has had to have his approval. And, he still doesn't trust me."

"Recently, we had a New Year's Eve party at our home with at least two dozen people invited. We had a small dance floor and a few of the guests asked me to dance, knowing how much I love to dance. Aidan sat in the back of the room seething with jealousy and let me know about it after the guests left, telling me not to have anything to do with any of those people again. These were married couples and their spouses didn't think anything of it, it was just a dance. It seemed so simple; he should have danced with me too. Why didn't he just come on the dance floor and say; It is my turn to dance with my girl."

"It has been many times like this that began to stack up over the years, and the time is now to let him go."

The attorney looked at Whitney with a somber expression and closed his eyes for a moment to gather his thoughts. Then he looked directly at Whitney and said, "Do you think your marriage may have failed because you aren't Jewish?"

Whitney fell back in the big chair, suddenly realizing how naïve she had been. Growing up in the country, she had never thought that people were all that different, but she was wrong, very wrong on this one.

She finally composed herself and replied, "I didn't know that he was Jewish. Aidan never expressed any belief in anything except himself. He has never practiced the Jewish faith, and he would often say that all religions were hogwash to him."

When Whitney thought about it, most if not all of his business associates were Jewish: Lewy in Grand Forks, Barney in Winnipeg, and so on and so on. But, that was the nature of his business and that didn't mean he was Jewish.

Whitney left the attorney's office with a blank expression on her face, thinking that she had been deceived all these years. Or, was she just that naïve? And she knew exactly what Aidan would say, "What difference does it make." But it did make a big difference. His heritage didn't allow for his wife to work outside of the home. A Jewish man is supposed to supply all his wife's needs, or he would not look successful. As his wife, you were the showcase of his success. At that moment, she remembered the time he drove her downtown to a furrier. "My girl needs to wear a mink coat when she is with me." He loved buying expensive trinkets or clothes for Whitney, and yet he would balk if she shopped for herself. "Take it back! It is not good enough for you." Whitney finally realized it was all about Aidan not making the purchase.

Aidan never took the time to see or ask who Whitney was, or what she wanted to do with her life. He had no idea how far she had come in her growth as a young woman, and he really never asked or cared how she felt or what she wanted. He just wanted her to be satisfied with the life role that he had envisioned for her. That meant she was to take care of the home while he was off doing what he always did. Whitney was supposed to alter how she lived, but Aidan never had any intention of changing.

Whitney often thought that Aidan had a girl on his arm, no matter where he traveled. Whitney was the secret girlfriend for a few years, so why wouldn't Aidan continue with someone else when he was away on business? No wonder he didn't trust Whitney. He himself didn't know what faithfulness was.

~

When Whitney left the attorneys' office that day, it was over, left only to memories of a few years in someone else's shoes; someone who appeared fearless, and who she wanted to stay close to, close to his magic and thirst for adventure like none she had ever known.

Whitney supposed it was somewhat like finding fools' gold: The overwhelming excitement, the rush of adrenaline, and then falling back into reality, and suddenly realizing, it was all a hoax.

~

Fool me once, shame on you; Fool me twice, shame on me.

From now on, she would hang on to the girl she knew that she really was.

Whitney had to tuck away a lifetime of adventure that was crammed into less than a decade. She knew she would never be the same. If she shared her story, most wouldn't believe her. If she was asked, "Where have you been these last years?" She would say; "Oh, here and there. But I am back now, and soon to be the Whitney you once knew."

She was on her way to start her life over again, and try once again to just be Whitney, the girl from the small town with grand ideas of seeing the world.

Be very careful what you wish for.

Thoughts are very powerful.

About the Author

Angie is a graduate of Metropolitan State University in St. Paul, MN., with a BA in Writing.

She lives in Minnesota

olsonangie8@gmail.com

Other books by the author:

Cecelia, Cause of Death

The Life of #8 Undisguised

Made in the USA
Middletown, DE
28 September 2024